"I don't expect you to drag up my past."

Then Gideon added huskily, "Which isn't to say that I don't want you to be very interested in my movements now."

She made herself smile at his teasing tone, not wanting him to guess how deeply her feelings were already involved with him. He smiled, not sensing her distress. "What are you going to do if I kiss you?"

Her mouth quirked. "Kiss you back?"

"I hope so," he said softly, moving to sit closer to her, one of his hands coming up to caress her cheek.

Laura was in a state of confusion. Did Gideon want an affair with her after all? And was her answer to be yes or no? She was very much afraid it was going to be yes. Afraid, because she was going to be hurt by such a relationship. But she would be hurt even more if she said no!

CAROLE MORTIMER
is also the author of these

Harlequin Presents

Many of these books are available at your local bookseller.

For a free catalog listing all titles currently available,
send your name and address to:

HARLEQUIN READER SERVICE
1440 South Priest Drive, Tempe, AZ 85281
Canadian address: Stratford, Ontario N5A 6W2

CAROLE MORTIMER

passion from the past

Harlequin Books

TORONTO • NEW YORK • LOS ANGELES • LONDON
AMSTERDAM • PARIS • SYDNEY • HAMBURG
STOCKHOLM • ATHENS • TOKYO • MILAN

For
John and Matthew

———————◆———————

Harlequin Presents first edition January 1983
ISBN 0-373-10564-9

Original hardcover edition published in 1982
by Mills & Boon Limited

CHAPTER ONE

'WHEW!' Janice collapsed down into the chair opposite Laura, her notebook dropping on to the desk in front of her. 'I think my fingers are going to fall off!' she groaned.

'Rough, was it?' Laura sympathised.

'Rough!' Janice leant back wearily. 'I didn't think so many people could all talk at the same time, and so fast too. I'll be glad when Dorothy gets back,' she moaned.

Dorothy Palmer was James Courtney's personal secretary, and Janice and Laura were her secretaries. But Dorothy had gone down with 'flu yesterday morning and had unwillingly been sent home, her last instruction being for Janice to sit in on the board meeting today and take the notes she usually took herself.

'She only went off yesterday,' Laura pointed out.

'She'll be back tomorrow, you can depend on it. In all the time I've been here I've never known Dorothy to take more than two days off, no matter how ill she is.' Janice bent over her notepad, grimacing. 'Now I've got to get these notes typed up before Mr Courtney starts screaming for them.'

'Would you like me to do it?' Laura instantly offered.

'No—thanks,' the other girl sighed. 'I'm going to have trouble reading it back myself—and I wrote it! I'll tell you what you could do for me, though. Mr Courtney would like a tray of coffee taken through to his office. Could you do that for me?'

Laura instantly stood up, smoothing down the straight skirt of her tailored black suit, a pale green blouse worn beneath the fitted jacket, her shoulder-length auburn hair secured with a tortoiseshell slide at her nape. She had taken to wearing the more mature clothing and severe hairstyle after being turned down for several jobs because of her youthful appearance. The clothes and hairstyle made her feel older than her nineteen years, giving her the confidence to try for this job at Courtneys. As her application and interview had been successful the image must have worked.

She had only been employed at Courtneys for three weeks, and so far she had had little to do with James Courtney himself, and the prospect of taking in his after-noon coffee, tea being preferred in the morning, filled her with apprehension.

'You know where to go, don't you?' Janice asked absently, her attention still on her hastily scribbled short-hand notes.

'I—Yes, I know.' Laura turned to go down to the executives' restaurant.

'I should call down first,' Janice advised. 'That way they'll have the coffee ready for when you get down there.'

'Oh yes, of course.' She picked up the telephone and dialled the number.

'Two cups,' Janice murmured, biting the end of her pencil. 'Mr Courtney has someone with him.'

Laura put the order in, hearing the flurry of activity when she told the girl the coffee was for Mr Courtney and smiled to herself as she went down the two floors in the lift. James Courtney had the effect of putting most people in a state of confusion, including herself, and she had no doubt the women in the canteen were even now rushing about preparing the fresh ground coffee Mr Courtney preferred, and putting a plate of his favourite chocolate biscuits on the tray too.

The first time she had collected his coffee tray she had been surprised by the presence of the biscuits, but she had been assured by Doreen in the canteen that Mr Courtney had a weakness for them. Laura found it difficult to think of that tall, distinguished man having any weaknesses at all; he always seemed like a very cold individual to her.

'Got a visitor today, has he?' Doreen asked conversationally as she handed over the tray.

'Yes,' Laura smiled.

'Dorothy not back yet?'

It was amazing how gossip spread about this firm. 'No,' she shook her head, not one who liked to gossip herself.

'Like working for Mr Courtney, do you?' Doreen probed.

'I—Yes.'

'Nice man,' Doreen nodded. 'A bit abrupt, but he knows what he wants. I like a man who knows what he wants.'

'I—Yes, he seems very nice,' Laura evaded; she found James Courtney more than 'a bit abrupt'. He frightened the life out of her every time he barked an order at her. But she didn't usually have a lot to do with him personally, thank goodness! If she worked directly for James Courtney she might not even have lasted the three weeks she had been here, Janice was senior, next to Dorothy, and so her own dealings with James Courtney kept to a minimum—and that was the way she liked it.

'I should take that up now,' Doreen advised curtly, obviously deciding she wasn't going to get much information out of Laura.

Laura flushed, making a hasty exit. Doreen had obviously expected to have a cosy little chat with her about Mr Courtney, most of his employees seeming to find this haughty man an interesting topic of conversation. Although what Doreen thought she could possibly relate about the man she just didn't know, James Courtney barely acknowledged her existence, let alone confided in her!

Janice glanced up as she entered their office. 'I should

take it through, he's buzzed for it twice already.'

Her face showed her dismay. 'But wouldn't you rather——'

'Don't ask me to take it in, Laura,' the other girl sighed impatiently. 'I'm up to my eyes with this typing. And he can't eat you,' she added derisively.

'He can try,' Laura grimaced.

'Go on in,' Janice laughed. 'If you let his coffee get cold he just might eat you at that!'

Laura swallowed hard, taking a deep breath before moving to knock on the inner office door. The abrupt 'enter' was not welcoming, and her hands shook as she picked the tray up to enter the room.

The two men inside instantly stopped talking, the one sitting in front of the desk rising politely to his feet, James Courtney remaining seated, obviously not considering his junior secretary worth the act of politeness. Laura eyed him nervously, finding him as daunting as she usually did, not sparing a glance in the other man's direction. James Courtney looked back at her broodingly, not welcoming her interruption at all.

In his early sixties, James Courtney was nevertheless still an attractive man, his thick hair iron grey, his face ruggedly lined, the eyes a pale blue, his mouth set in its usual thin line. Laura couldn't ever remember seeing him smile, although surely no one could be this grim all the time.

She looked down at the desk, searching for a space to put the tray down. There didn't appear to be one.

'Let me,' a deep voice remarked from behind her, and the man moved forward to move some of the papers aside.

Laura gratefully put the heavy tray down, and turned to thank the man. The words caught and held in her throat, as she found herself looking at the most devastatingly handsome man she had ever seen in her young life, his slate grey eyes widening as she continued to stare at him.

But she couldn't have looked away if her life had depended upon it, feeling almost mesmerised, caught in a spell she had no will or wish to break. This man was taller even than James Courtney, being at least a foot taller than her own five feet two inches. He was a man in his mid-thirties, with a lean ripcord body that oozed power and determination, his face even more powerful as he continued to meet her wide-eyed stare. His eyes seemed to be constantly changing colour, at one moment a light silver, at others almost black. His nose was long and straight, his mouth jutting out determinedly above the strong jaw, his skin deeply tanned. The dark suit fitted him perfectly, the snowy white shirt emphasising the deep tan on his face and strong, tapered hands.

Laura couldn't ever remember noticing so much about one person on first sight before, finding herself fascinated by the deep cleft in his chin, the way his dark hair grew thickly over his collar, styled casually back from his face, the face she couldn't look away from. It was as if time suddenly stood still, allowing her to look her fill of this man she felt captivated by. And she didn't ever want to stop looking at him.

She knew it was stupid, knew that a man of the thirty-five-thirty-six she guessed him to be was probably married with a couple of children, that he wouldn't be interested in her even if he weren't married, and yet her attraction to him was so strong the rest of the world had ceased to exist.

But her silent admiration of him couldn't last, she had known it couldn't, and finally he was the one to break it.

'Thank you, Miss——?' He looked at her enquiringly.

His voice was as fascinating as the rest of him, deep and husky, and she shivered with excitement as she wondered how it would feel to have such a man make love to her. She blushed scarlet at the intimacy of her

thoughts, groaning inwardly as she realised how the tide
of red colour would clash with her auburn hair.

Heavens, she must be making a prize idiot of herself,
standing here goggle-eyed about a perfect stranger.
'Jamieson,' she supplied jerkily, cursing herself for the way
her voice quivered.

'Jamieson?' he echoed softly.

'I—er—Yes, sir,' she licked her lips nervously, 'Laura
Jamieson.'

'That will be all, Miss Jamieson.' James Courtney spoke
to her for the first time since she had entered the room,
his voice curt.

She blushed anew. 'Er—yes, sir.' She turned to flee the
room, aware that she had made more of a fool of herself
in front of the older man than she usually did.

'And tell your colleague to hurry with those notes,' he
snapped. 'Dorothy doesn't usually keep me waiting this
length of time.'

'Er—no, sir.' Now she was sounding like the idiot she
was acting! But James Courtney couldn't know that
Dorothy didn't usually keep him waiting because she had
Janice and herself do the typing for her.

She liked Dorothy immensely, and found the older
woman kind and helpful, the three of them working very
well together in their spacious office. As James Courtney's
personal secretary it was only right that she should pass
on the more mundane task of typing to her juniors, her
other duties time consuming enough.

She hurried from the room, aware that the two men
had already dismissed her from their minds as they
resumed their conversation. She closed the door behind
her with a sigh, realising that she was trembling, her hands
shaking almost incontrollably. That man, a man whose
name she didn't even know, had affected her more deeply
than any person she had ever met.

Janice looked up from her typing. 'All right, love?' she

asked concernedly. 'You're looking a little pale—you aren't coming down with the 'flu too, are you? I've heard the whole company is getting it.'

'I—No, I—I feel fine.' She moved to the seat behind her desk. 'That man—the man with Mr Courtney, who is he?'

Janice shrugged. 'One of the board members, I suppose. At the end of the meeting Mr Courtney just said coffee for two in his office, I couldn't tell you who was going to be with him. What does he look like? I should be able to tell you his name if you describe him to me.' She grimaced. 'Most of them are distinguishable.'

That strong, arrogant face instantly came back into her mind, each sharp angle, each hard feature vividly imprinted in her memory—and her heart?

She pushed that disturbing thought to the back of her mind. She had made enough of a fool of herself for one day without imagining that mind-shattering attraction she had experienced was love. Love came slowly, with familiarity, not in a fraction of a second, and not with a complete stranger.

'Well?' Janice prompted, eager to get on with her work.

Laura forced herself to make the description rationally. 'Very tall, dark, with grey eyes. Oh—and he has a deep tan, as if he's just been on holiday.'

Janice smiled, nodding. 'He has.'

'He has?'

'Mm,' the other girl nodded again. 'He got back the day before yesterday, from the Bahamas. The man you've just described is Gideon Maitland.'

Gideon—his name was Gideon. 'Oh?' She tried to sound casual in her interest, but knew she had failed when Janice smiled sympathetically.

'Don't worry,' she consoled, 'we've all been through it.'

'Through what?' Laura asked resentfully.

'Falling in love with Gideon Maitland.' Janice sighed. 'Not that it got any of us anywhere. He just isn't interested, not in the likes of us anyway.'

'I'm not in love with him,' Laura said indignantly. 'I just—Well, he—I just wondered who he was. Does he work here? I've never seen him before.' She would have remembered him if she had.

'I told you, he's been in the Bahamas. And he more than works here, he's being groomed to take over as chairman when Mr Courtney retires next year.'

Laura couldn't help her look of surprise. 'Isn't he a little young for that? Surely Mr McNee is next in seniority?'

'Next in age, you mean,' Janice grinned. 'But Mr McNee isn't Mr Courtney's son-in-law, Gideon Maitland is.'

'I didn't know Mr Courtney had a daughter,' Laura gasped. She hadn't even realised he had been married, let alone that he had children. With this knowledge Gideon Maitland moved even farther out of her orbit—if he had ever entered it!

'He doesn't, not any more.' Janice shrugged. 'She died a couple of years ago.'

'Oh, how terrible!' Laura's sympathy was sincere, even though a few seconds ago she hadn't even known the other woman existed. It was always tragic to hear of a death, especially as the other woman couldn't have been all that old, mid-thirties at most. She shook her head. 'No wonder Mr Maitland isn't interested in women.'

'I didn't say that,' Janice snorted. 'I just said he wasn't interested in office girls. Now actresses are a different matter.'

Laura looked startled. 'Actresses?'

'Well, one actress in particular, actually. You've heard of Petra Wilde, haven't you?'

A mental image of the sultry actress instantly sprang to

mind. Tall, with hair the colour of ebony, her eyes the aquamarine of a clear sea, the other woman was spectacularly beautiful, admired as much for that perfect beauty as she was for her splendid acting.

'When she won her Oscar last year,' Janice related with relish. 'Guess who was there with her?'

'Gideon Mailtand,' Laura said dully.

'Mm,' Janice nodded excitedly. 'There've been rumours of them going to marry for months, although I doubt it will happen now. Maybe she isn't the maternal type. After all, not many women would be willing to take on another woman's child.'

'What child?' Laura frowned her puzzlement, feeling as if she had lost Janice somewhere in this conversation.

'Gideon Maitland has a little girl. Didn't I explain that? No, I don't suppose I did. Well, Gideon and Felicity—that's Mr Courtney's daughter—were married for ten years before she became pregnant. I think Mr Courtney had just about given up on them. Anyway, she finally became pregnant, and then she died during the birth. The baby almost died too.'

'But Felicity—Mr Maitland's wife died?' It sounded a terrible tragedy to her.

'Yes,' Janice nodded; she was a pretty blonde in her late twenties, just waiting for the right man to come along so that she could give up work and have his children. 'I think Natalie is about eighteen months old now, so Felicity died that long ago. I can still remember Mr Courtney's face when he came in to work the next day. He looked as if his whole world had fallen apart. He lost his wife the same way, you know.'

'And—and Mr Maitland? How did he react? He must have been shattered, losing his wife like that when they'd waited so long to have a child.'

'Hard to say,' Janice shrugged. 'He didn't come back to work for a couple of months, and by that time I suppose the worst of it was over. Although he had changed,' she added thoughtfully. 'He became even more withdrawn into himself. Not that he'd ever been the chatty type, but at least he used to say good morning once in a while. Now he barely notices your existence.'

'It must have been hard for him,' Laura excused, feeling Gideon Maitland's pain as if it were her own. 'I'm sure it can't have been all that easy bringing up a baby on his own, especially as it's a little girl.'

Janice gave a scornful snort. 'Men like Gideon Maitland can afford to pay people to bring up their children for them.'

'Oh, but surely——'

'Natalie has a nanny to take care of her, a friend of the family, so I've heard. Gideon Maitland is reputed not to have a lot of time for her.'

'He probably blames the little girl for the death of his wife.'

'Probably,' Janice agreed. 'But I——'

'Miss Lawson!' James Courtney's voice came clearly over the intercom.

Janice pulled a face at Laura, moving to answer him. 'Yes, sir?'

'Are those notes typed up yet?' he rasped.

'Er—almost,' she invented.

'Bring them in as soon as they're finished.' The intercom was switched off.

Janice wrinkled her nose. 'What does he think I'm going to do with them?' she said dryly.

Laura laughed. 'He just isn't a patient man.'

'Neither is Gideon Maitland,' Janice was obviously enjoying talking about him, especially to the newcomer Laura was.

Laura looked down at her desk. 'What's his daughter like?'

The other girl shrugged. 'I've never seen her. But if

she's anything like her mother then she's lovely. Felicity Maitland was the most beautiful woman I've ever seen.'

Laura's eyes were wide. 'More beautiful even than Petra Wilde?'

'Much more,' Janice nodded. 'She was tall and blonde, and very sophisticated. She used to make me feel like a dowd every time she came to the office.'

Considering how attractive Janice's blonde beauty was Laura knew that the other woman must have been exquisite. She always felt inadequate when in the company of such women, her childish features set in a heart-shaped face, her huge green eyes seeming to dominate her other features, her nose small and snub, her mouth slightly tilted at the corners, her little chin had a determined tilt to it, a determination that was rarely asserted, although once she was roused to temper anything might happen. No doubt Felicity Maitland had had a good dress sense too, whereas she dressed to look efficient at the office in an effort to make up for her obvious youth, the tailored suits and fitted blouses worn for effect rather than style or elegance.

Right now she felt the dowd Janice said she usually felt, even the brightness of her hair dulled by its confinement. A man like Gideon Maitland wouldn't even spare her a second glance, if indeed he had spared her a first one, and she was a fool for wishing he would.

She bent over her typewriter as she heard him taking his leave of James Courtney, the two men obviously arranging to meet at Gideon's house later that evening, possibly for dinner.

She couldn't stop herself, she just had to look up, to catch one last glimpse of him. After all, there was no saying when she would get to see him again, he had been back two days already and this was the first she had seen of him. He was just striding past their open office door, those grey eyes flickering over her coldly before he looked away again, James Courtney's little mouse of a junior secretary dismissed from his mind—if she had ever entered it!

'Miss Lawson!' James Courtney had obviously reached the end of what little patience he possessed, his voice over the intercom chillier than ever.

'God, what a bear!' Janice frantically collected up the disordered typewritten sheets.

'I'd better get on too,' Laura grimaced. 'He'll want these letters for signing before he leaves at five.'

But her mind wasn't on what she was doing, her usually faultless typing having a few errors today. Her secretarial qualifications were excellent, she wouldn't have been employed at Courtneys if they weren't, but when she had attained these qualifications she hadn't had to contend with piercing grey eyes looking back at her from the keyboard of her typewriter, or to see Gideon Maitland's hard face every time she glanced at her notepad.

The man was haunting her, his hard face was constantly on her mind. And it just wasn't like her. She very rarely dated, spending most of her evenings at home, usually with her widowed mother, both of them missing her brother Martin. He had gone to America to work two years ago, claiming that there were more opportunities over there. And there did seem to be, his rapid advancement in the advertising company he had gone to work for seeming to prove his point.

Even through her preoccupation with Gideon Maitland Laura could see her mother's excitement when she got home later that evening, guessing the reason to be the long-awaited letter from Martin. Her brother was notoriously bad at writing letters, and their mother couldn't understand why she only received replies to one in every four letters she wrote him. Laura was more inclined to make excuses for him, continuing to write to him even though he rarely replied, knowing that he had a demanding job, and an even more demanding social life, a constant stream of girls seeming to pass through his life.

'Yet another girl-friend!' her mother tutted disapprovingly. 'I don't think he'll ever settle down and give me grandchildren. You'll probably marry before he does.'

Laura snorted at the unlikelihood of that, looking about sixteen now that she had changed out of her work clothes and released her hair. It splayed across her shoulders in natural waves, the colour now a deep rich red, her loose-fitting tee-shirt a pale green, her denims old and faded.

'How's his work going?' she asked interestedly.

'You know Martin,' her mother dismissed, obviously reading the letter for about the tenth time. 'Ever the optimist. He thinks there's a chance he could be made a partner in the near future.'

That sounded like Martin. He was very like their father had been, always craving change, new excitement. He had worked for Courtneys a couple of years ago, and it was because he had said what a good company they were to work for that Laura had applied for the job there. And he had been proven correct; Courtneys were a good company to work for, very good to their staff.

They needed to be over the next few days, as the majority of the staff went down with 'flu, Janice among them.

The day she worked for Mr Courtney on her own was the worst day she had known since her employment here. He was a brute of a man to work for, and how Dorothy coped with him all the time she had no idea. He allowed no respite for the fact that instead of his usual three secretaries he was now reduced to just his very junior secretary, demanding the same efficiency from her that he usually got from a full staff.

Her coffee-break went by the board as he dictated letters to her in his quick decisive manner; luckily her shorthand speed fast enough to keep up with him. Her lunch-break had to be given a miss too, as the telephone rang constantly and prevented her typing the letters.

'Not finished yet, Miss Jamieson?' he came back from his own lunch to bark at her.

'Er—no——'

'Then it's about time you were,' he snapped.

'Yes, sir——' Her fingers hit three wrong keys in succession as he stood glowering over her.

James Courtney scowled at her mistakes. 'At this rate you won't finish before the end of the week, let alone the end of the day!'

'I—Oh dear!' Laura groaned as she made yet another mistake. If only he wouldn't stand over her like this, completely unnerving her.

'Good God, girl,' he exploded, his craggy face lined with anger, 'you can't even type!'

'Of course I can type,' she heard herself retorting. 'You wouldn't have employed me if I couldn't. It's just that——'

'Excuses, excuses,' he dismissed tersely. 'If you aren't up to the work, Miss Jamieson, then perhaps I ought to employ someone who is.'

Normally she would have agreed with him and got on with her work. But it had been a hard, difficult week, and she was feeling tired and hungry, the toast and coffee she had gulped down for her breakfast seeming a very long time ago.

So James Courtney had chosen the wrong day to take his temper out on her, and the temper that went with her shade of hair, and was so rarely used by her, for once got the better of her. She looked up at him with sparkling green eyes. 'I'm up to the work, Mr Courtney,' she told him tautly. '*My* work,' she added with emphasis. 'It may have escaped your notice, but I happen to be working alone here.'

His eyes widened, obviously unaccustomed to his employees answering him back in this way. 'Where's Miss Lawson?' he demanded tersely.

'She's off with the 'flu,' Laura blushed as she realised how she had just spoken to her employer. She couldn't ever remember talking to anyone like that before. But then she couldn't ever remember anyone being that rude to her before either. She looked down at her hands, slender, capable hands, the nails kept short for her work. 'I did tell you this morning, Mr Courtney,' she added huskily.

He scowled heavily, his dark brows low over his icy blue eyes. 'Half the damned company is off with 'flu. I suppose you'll get it next,' he snapped accusingly, before going into his office and closing the door firmly behind him.

Considering he had more or less told her she was incompetent she was surprised that the prospect of her being off work should bother him. What a bad-tempered old man he was!

Tears filled her eyes, and she buried her face in her hands as she wept. She had been trying so hard to please him, had thought she was succeeding, and with a few biting words he had shown her exactly what he thought of her efforts.

'Is there anything wrong?'

She looked up with a start, to find herself looking straight at Gideon Maitland, the dark brown suit and cream shirt he wore seeming to make his tan appear even darker. She gulped as he came into the office, reaching frantically into her handbag for a tissue to blow her nose, wiping away the telltale tears at the same time.

' 'Flu?' he enquired softly, his voice as rich and deep as she remembered.

He was all just as she remembered him, every virile inch of him!

And once again she was making an idiot of herself. Why couldn't she just act normally about him for once? 'I—er—no.' She took her compact out of her bag, viewing her reflection in the mirror with distaste. Heavens, no

wonder he thought she had a cold, with her puffed eyes
and red nose that was exactly what it looked like! She
hastily closed the compact, knowing she couldn't make
the necessary repairs to her face in front of this man. 'I
think I must have had something in my eye,' she
invented.

Gideon Maitland's mouth twisted, as if he knew very
well that the 'something' had been tears. 'Is James back
from lunch yet?'

She nodded, glad he didn't pursue the subject of her
tears. 'He came back several minutes ago,' she confirmed.

'I see.' He pursed his lips. 'And would he be the—er—
reason you had something in your eye?' Dark eyebrows
rose over light grey eyes.

Colour flooded her cheeks. 'I—er—Yes.' The question
came as too much of a surprise for her to prevaricate.

His handsome mouth twisted with humour. 'His lunch
obviously didn't sweeten his temper.'

Laura licked her lips nervously. What was she supposed
to say to a comment like that! 'I wouldn't know, Mr
Maitland,' she replied demurely.

He didn't seem surprised that she knew his name; he
leaned back easily against her desk, his arms folded across
his chest. 'That's very loyal of you,' he drawled. 'Your
lunch obviously agreed with you.'

'I didn't——' She bit her lip, her lashes fluttering up,
only to lower quickly again as her green eyes clashed with
clear grey ones.

'Didn't what?' Gideon Maitland probed sharply.

'Nothing,' she shook her head. 'I'll tell Mr Courtney
you're here,' and she moved to press the intercom.

Long tapered fingers came out to stop her. 'Didn't
what?' Gideon Maitland requested firmly.

Laura extracted her hand from his, her heart fluttering
wildly in her chest from the contact. 'I—I haven't had
time for lunch. You see——'

He stood up. 'Go and have some now,' he ordered briskly.

'There's really no need——'

'There's every need, Miss Jamieson,' he told her coldly. 'Lack of food is apt to lower your resistance to infection. The last thing James needs is to have no secretary at all.'

That put her firmly in her place—even an incompetent secretary was better than none at all! 'I'll go now,' she said jerkily. 'If you'll just explain to Mr Courtney . . .'

He nodded curtly and moved impatiently to the door that connected her office to James Courtney's. 'I'll do that,' he told her abruptly.

She grabbed her handbag and almost ran out of the office, having once again found Gideon Maitland completely overwhelming.

Her hand trembled as she sat alone in the canteen drinking her coffee. There had been a coldness about him, a bitter twist to his beautiful mouth. And no wonder, he probably still missed his wife very much.

And Petra Wilde? Well, he was a man, she shrugged, and men had—appetites, especially if they had been married. Her cheeks coloured delicately as she realised her thoughts had taken her to Gideon Maitland's bed. A shiver of delight ran down her spine as she imagined those strong, sensitive hands making love to her.

Heavens, she was acting like an infatuated adolescent, fantasising about the latest pop or film-star! But it was more than that, she knew it was. She felt so attracted to him, so aware of him, as if she had always been waiting for such a man. A pity he hadn't always been waiting for a redheaded, green-eyed nineteen-year-old!

It was good that she could still laugh at herself, as no doubt Gideon Maitland was laughing at her. He was experienced enough with women to know what her reaction to him meant. If only she could stop this childish trembling every time he came near her, and the way she stuttered and stumbled over her words was so juvenile.

She didn't even know if he was still in with James Courtney when she returned from eating her sandwich lunch, as the walls of the inner office were soundproofed. Her own office still contained the aroma of the cheroot he had been smoking, and the tangy smell was pleasant to the senses, his aftershave masculine and spicy.

Was there nothing she disliked about the man! Yes, of course there was, she told herself crossly, she just didn't know him well enough to say what they were. His eyes were cold, for one thing, cold and assessing, and he had a cynical twist to his lips constantly, mockery or boredom seeming to be his two main expressions.

She shouldn't be thinking about him now, she should be thinking of the work she still had to do before she could go home tonight. And goodness knows, there was enough of it!

She was pounding away on her typewriter when the communicating door opened and Gideon Maitland strolled out of the main office. Laura sighed heavily as she hit the wrong key. Her typing teacher would have a fit if she could see the mess she was making of her work today— first James Courtney unnerving her and now Gideon Maitland! She back-spaced and corrected her mistake, half listening to the two men's conversation without really meaning to. But when Gideon Maitland mentioned her name she found herself more than half listening.

'I'll see your Miss Jamieson on Monday morning, then,' he drawled.

'First thing,' the other man nodded.

That perfect mouth twisted derisively. 'I'm sure Miss Jamieson is never late.'

Chilling blue eyes swept over her rigid figure as she could only make a pretence of typing. 'Are you, Gideon?' James Courtney clipped. 'I can't say keeping an eye on

Miss Jamieson's timekeeping has exactly occupied any of my thoughts.'

Her mouth tightened as the two men seemed to taunt her without actually talking to her directly. And what did Gideon Maitland mean, he would see him on Monday morning?

'I'm sure it hasn't.' He was smiling openly now, his teeth very white and even against his tan, suddenly looking years younger than the thirty-five years she knew him to be.

James Courtney gave him a considering look. 'Has it occupied any of yours?'

The other man's expression at once became bland. 'Not that I recall,' he replied distantly.

'Sure?' Once again those light blue eyes flickered over Laura.

'Very sure,' Gideon Maitland said tightly. 'Will you be over to see Natalie tomorrow?' he firmly changed the subject.

'Of course.' The other man's voice was gruff.

Gideon Maitland nodded curtly. 'I'll tell her to expect you.'

'I thought I might take her to the Zoo.'

'She'll like that,' he nodded.

Laura tried to envisage James Courtney entertaining his granddaughter at the Zoo, and failed miserably. She couldn't see him anywhere other than seated behind his huge mahogany desk, master of all he surveyed.

She chided herself for being unfair. The man obviously thought a lot of his daughter's child—he had to if he was willing to take her to the Zoo!

'Finished yet, Miss Jamieson?'

Lord, she wished he would stop pouncing on her like that! She had been trying to imagine him in the role of doting grandparent, and during that time Gideon Maitland seemed to have taken his leave.

'Almost,' she was relieved to be able to answer.

He continued to stare at her, not moving back into his own office as she had expected him to. 'My son-in-law tells me I've been working you too hard,' he said mildly.

Colour flooded her cheeks. 'Oh no,' she shook her head. 'You——'

'Oh yes,' he insisted. 'What do you have to say about that?'

'Why, nothing,' she gasped. 'I——'

'Nothing?' he pounced. 'Then you don't agree with him?'

'Well, I—I——'

'You do!' A grim smile of satisfaction lightened his features.

'Not really,' she evaded his piercing eyes. 'I—We've all been busy lately, I've worked no harder than anyone else.'

'Exactly what I told Gideon,' he nodded. 'Well, we'll see which one of us you consider a slavedriver after Monday.'

'Sir?' she eyed him questioningly.

A ghost of a smile lightened his harsh features. 'I can assure you that Gideon is even more difficult to work for than I am.'

Laura frowned, having no idea what this man was talking about. Whatever it was it seemed to amuse him.

'Dorothy will be back on Monday,' he informed her curtly, obviously tiring of being amused at her expense. 'You're to report to Gideon at nine o'clock Monday morning. His secretary has gone down with this damned 'flu bug—and you're to be her replacement.'

CHAPTER TWO

'IT's a wonderful opportunity for you!' Laura's mother exclaimed when told of the arrangements for Monday morning.

'But I already work for the chairman of the company,' Laura sighed. 'I can't get any higher than that.'

'You're only his junior secretary, dear,' her mother said dismissively. 'And besides, you said this Gideon Maitland is going to be made chairman next year when James Courtney steps down.'

'Steps down' didn't quite apply to the way Laura expected James Courtney to relinquish his control of Courtneys. She had no doubt that he would be about for years to come, that although he might be willing to appear to give control to his son-in-law that there would one day be quite a power struggle between the two men. James Courtney would still be capable of running the firm when he was eighty, she had no doubt of that.

'He is,' she confirmed her mother's statement. 'But filling in for his secretary when she's off sick isn't exactly what I'd planned for my future.'

'Don't be silly, dear!' Her mother's tone was impatient, the red of Laura's hair a deep chestnut on the older woman, her face and figure still youthfully attractive. 'When he's made chairman, if you've made enough of an impression on him, then he may just make you his personal secretary.'

Laura knew her mother was ambitious for her, in fact it had been her mother's promptings that had made her apply for the senior position she already had at Courtneys, but surely even she couldn't imagine she could be made

27

personal secretary to the chairman of a company as big as
Courtneys at the age of twenty, as she would be next
year? It appeared she could.

'There are plenty of other girls more qualified for the
position,' she pointed out to her mother. 'The girl I'm
standing in for on Monday, for one.'

'I've no doubt she is.' Her mother's eyebrows rose. 'But
you'll just have to make yourself even more—indispens-
able to him, won't you?'

Laura frowned, looking at her mother disbelievingly.
'What do you mean?'

'Oh, don't be naïve, Laura!' Her mother stood up to
pace the room impatiently. 'No girl gets anywhere these
days on qualifications alone, there are just too many
talented women. I've no doubt Gideon Maitland's present
secretary makes more than her secretarial attributes
available to him.'

'Mother!' Laura gasped her indignation on the other
girl's behalf. 'Diane Holland is happily married.'

'So?'

'Mother, really!' And Laura left the room in disgust,
going upstairs to her bedroom before she lost her temper.

Where her mother got these ridiculous ideas from she
just didn't know, but this one about Gideon Maitland
was the most ridiculous yet. Her mother couldn't really
imagine she would enter into an affair with a man just to
get on in her career. No woman had to do that nowadays.
It was the time of equality, wasn't it?

Besides which, she had no reason to suppose Gideon
Maitland had even realised she was female, let alone that
he was attracted to her. Goodness, a man like that, with
his looks and money, could take his pick of any woman in
the world. Hadn't he chosen the beautiful and famous
Petra Wilde to be his girl-friend?—and they didn't come
any more exclusively beautiful than that. Gideon
Maitland had no need to indulge in needless affairs with

his secretary. Why cause complications like that in his
office when he had the lovely Petra Wilde in his life—in
his bed?

Nevertheless, her mother had put the thought in her
mind, and consequently she felt awkward about facing
Gideon Maitland on Monday morning. Not that he could
possibly know about the embarrassing suggestion her
mother had made, but she knew, and she could hardly
bear to face him.

She arrived early on Monday morning, her intention
being to explain the work of the past week to Dorothy
before she had to go down the corridor to Gideon
Maitland's office. Dorothy always arrived at eight-thirty,
so Laura had decided to do the same this morning,
spending the next half an hour going over every detail of the work she had done in the other woman's ab-
sence.

When she had finished she gave Dorothy a shy smile.
'It's good to have you back.'

The other woman smiled, a woman in her mid-forties
who had been with James Courtney for the last twenty
years. It was rumoured that she had been in love with her
boss years ago, but her sudden marriage at the age of
forty seemed to have put an end to that. But her loyalty to
James Courtney remained constant even during his cruel-
lest of moods—and he had plenty of those.

'Mr Courtney doesn't like his routine disturbed,'
Dorothy excused, as if guessing that he had been unbear-
able to work for the last few days. 'You'll find Mr
Maitland a lot less—strict about the rules.'

In other words he wasn't such a swine to work for!
Even guessing how impossible their bad-tempered boss
had been the last few days Dorothy could still defend him.
And no doubt his mood would mellow now that his efficient, almost mind-reading secretary was back.

Laura stood up reluctantly. 'I suppose I'd better go

along to Mr Maitland's office now, it's almost nine.'

Dorothy was sorting through the pile of mail on her desk, already back in command. 'Good luck, dear,' she said absently. 'And if you run into any problems don't hesitate to call me for help, although you should find the work more or less the same as here.'

'I hope so,' Laura said fervently.

She had no choice but to go to Gideon Maitland's office now, remembering his comment about her not being late.

The door to the inner office was closed, so she assumed he was already in there. Now what did she do? His secretary's desk seemed to be clear of all visible work, but she couldn't just sit here doing nothing.

'Good morning.'

She turned with a start, blushing as she saw Gideon Maitland standing casually in the doorway of his office. 'Good morning—er, sir,' she returned awkwardly.

He straightened, very dark and attractive in a navy blue three-piece suit, the waistcoat fitted against his taut stomach. Most men of his age, seated behind a desk all day, would have run to fat by now, but this man obviously had some way of keeping fit. The memory of Petra Wilde and his relationship with her instantly flashed into Laura's mind, and she blushed at her own awareness of this man's attraction. He made her quiver all over just to look at him, and how she was going to work with him she had no idea.

'Call me Gideon,' he invited smoothly.

'Oh no,' she shook her head, wishing she had more confidence in her appearance. Once again she was dressed to look cool and efficient, the brown tailored suit and cream blouse were smart if not exactly attractive. 'I—I couldn't.'

'Of course you could,' he insisted briskly. 'I have every intention of calling you Laura.'

She flushed with the pleasure of him actually being

aware of her first name. 'That's different.'

His mouth twisted. 'Because I'm the boss and you're the secretary?'

'Well, I—Yes.' She looked down at her hands.

Gideon looked at her steadily, his piercing grey eyes taking in everything about her. 'We may not always have just a business relationship,' he drawled.

Laura swallowed hard, looking at him with wide eyes. Goodness, her mother couldn't be right, could she? This man wouldn't expect more than secretarial duties from her, would he? Not that she wasn't attracted to him, but she didn't approve of those types of relationships. Besides, he had Petra Wilde, hadn't he? No, he must just mean that perhaps they could become friends. She would like that.

'What would you like me to do, Mr Maitland—er— Gideon?' It didn't feel right calling him that, and she doubted she would be able to do it again.

The morning rushed by in a haze of work. Gideon Maitland was as dynamic as James Courtney, although he wasn't so aggressive to the people he worked with, making sure she went to lunch even though they were really busy. Laura enjoyed working with him, and found him decisive and accurate, quick to put people down if they made a mistake but equally quick to give praise if praise were due.

For all the wall of harshness that surrounded him he was popular with the other staff, male and female alike, and most of them could hardly wait for the time he took over as chairman.

'I wouldn't mind being his secretary,' one of the girls at Laura's table remarked as she ate her lunch in the staff canteen. Gideon Maitland was up in the executives' dining-room—and not, Laura felt sure, eating a ham salad either.

Laura shrugged. 'He's very nice to work for.' She wasn't

going to get into a discussion about him, feeling a loyalty towards him after only one morning of working for him.

'Who wants to work?' the other girl laughed; she was secretary to one of the department managers.

Laura blushed. 'Mr Maitland works very hard,' she defended, and gulped down her coffee, anxious to leave.

'He plays very hard too,' Susan grinned. 'There's a photograph of him in my magazine this week,' she bent to take it out of her handbag. 'He's with Petra Wilde.' She found the appropriate page and spread the magazine out in front of Laura.

Laura didn't want to look, hadn't wanted to see how well Gideon and the beautiful actress looked together. And they did look good, as she had known they would. Petra Wilde was almost as tall as her escort, her flaming red dress daring in the extreme as the two of them attended the premiere of the actress's latest film. Gideon Maitland was laughing down at the other woman, looking happy and relaxed, completely unlike the harsh man he was during working hours. He looked so tall and distinguished, the photograph showing the wings of grey at his temples, his magnificent physique shown to full advantage in the black evening suit and snowy white shirt.

No wonder Petra Wilde gazed up at him so adoringly, her blue eyes sparkling with some secret message. The couple's whole relationship looked intimate, Gideon's arm firmly about the actress's waist as he held her at his side.

'Very nice,' Laura pushed the magazine back across the table to Susan. 'It's a very good photograph,' she added as she saw the other girl's disappointed expression at her reaction.

'You don't seem very interested, I must say,' Susan said in a disgruntled voice.

If the other girl knew what a wrench the photograph gave to her heart she wouldn't say that. Laura had expected to have her romantic illusions about Gideon destroyed once she began working for him, had thought the familiarity would show her how silly her infatuation was, but if anything she had fallen more under his spell, gazing at him longingly when he wasn't looking at her.

'I have to get back.' She stood up, knowing that she still had twenty minutes of her lunch-break left, but not prepared to sit and answer questions about Gideon for all that time.

As she had thought, her new boss was still out at lunch when she got back, but she could use this time to finish her typing.

'That's what I like to see.'

She looked up to see Nigel Jennings, the Personnel Manager for the company, standing in the open doorway. She returned his smile as he came over to her desk. 'What's that?' she asked.

'Well, I must have made the right decision when I employed you,' he grinned, sitting on the edge of her desk. 'Otherwise you wouldn't be working for Gideon.'

'It's only temporary.'

He nodded; he was a man of about thirty, with boyishly blond good looks. He looked too young to carry the responsibilities he did, and yet Laura knew James Courtney valued his work, that he trusted his judgement implicitly. The only time he seemed to have doubted his judgement had been in Nigel's employment of her!

'Diane's off with 'flu.' He picked up the paperweight from the desk. 'But then so is almost everyone else.' He grimaced. 'That's why I'm here to see Gideon, actually. It's the firm's annual dinner-dance next week, and if half the company isn't going to be able to go it might be better if we just cancelled it.'

'I suppose so.' Laura had forgotten all about the dinner-dance, and in any case had not intended going even if she did manage to evade catching this 'flu bug that was running rife in the company.

Nigel quirked an eyebrow at her. 'I suppose you're bringing your boy-friend along?'

'Well, actually——'

'You aren't?' he cut in eagerly.

Laura viewed him with something like dismay, guessing that his reaction when she told him she wasn't thinking of going would be to invite her to go with him. Not that she didn't like him, on the few occasions when they had spoken together she had found him a very agreeable companion. But she knew from experience what these company dinners were like, knew the romantic speculation that would go on for days afterwards if two employees spent any time together at all.

'I'm not going. You see,' she added firmly as he made to protest, 'I don't like to leave my mother alone in the evenings. She's a widow, and——'

'Surely one night isn't going to hurt,' Nigel protested, his open features clearly showing his disappointment. 'It isn't as if it happens every night of the week. And I'd like you to come. Laura——'

'Hello, Nigel.' Gideon Maitland had miraculously appeared in the office, not that he could possibly know the embarrassment he was saving her if she had had to turn down Nigel's invitation. Grey eyes flickered coldly, over them both, and Nigel slowly stood up. 'Anything I can do for you?' Gideon asked politely enough. 'Or did you just come to see my secretary?' His voice hardened perceptively.

The other man flushed, obviously as unnerved by this tall imposing man as everyone else seemed to be. 'I came to see you, actually, Gideon.' He had obviously recovered his composure. 'But——'

'But while you were here you thought you'd chat up my secretary,' Gideon drawled.

'I—Well——'

'Come through to my office,' Gideon instructed briskly.

'Are you back from lunch, Laura?'

'Er—yes, sir.'

He nodded, his face darkening at her formal way of addressing him. Laura waited until the two men had gone through to the other office before restarting her typing. It felt strange to hear Gideon keep referring to her as 'his secretary' when all she was doing was filling in for a few days. As soon as Diane was back she would return to James Courtney's tyranny.

Gideon had been angry about her talking to Nigel, and he had every right to be. She might still have been on her lunch-break at the time, but the conversation had taken place in the office, a social conversation that he had every right to object to.

Nigel came out of the office about ten minutes later. 'About next week, Laura——'

'Laura, could you come in here, please,' Gideon requested curtly from behind him. 'Was there anything else, Nigel?' he looked calmly at the other man.

Nigel shrugged his defeat in the face of a determination stronger than his own. 'No, nothing. Perhaps I'll see you for lunch tomorrow, Laura?'

'I—Perhaps.' She was already gathering up her shorthand pad and pencil, one look at Gideon's face telling her that he wasn't in a mood to be kept waiting.

She walked proudly past Gideon as he pointedly held the door open to his office, and sat down in the chair opposite his, her pencil poised expectantly, looking up uncertainly as he seemed in no hurry to begin dictation.

'Are you in the habit of spending time with Nigel Jennings?' he asked suddenly.

Laura blinked dazedly at the unexpectedness of such a question, her notepad slowly lowering to her knees. 'I beg your pardon?' she frowned.

'Out of working hours you're free to see who you want,' he continued harshly. 'But while you're working for me I would prefer it if you saw your boy-friend away from my office.'

'Nigel—I mean, Mr Jennings isn't my boy-friend!' she gasped indignantly.

Gideon raised dark eyebrows. 'He isn't?'

'No. He came up here to see you, not me.'

'I see. Do you have a boy-friend?'

'Why?' she asked the question without thinking, blushing at the look of irritation that passed across his handsome face. 'I mean——'

'You mean why do I want to know about your personal life,' he drawled, relaxing back in his chair. He shrugged. 'I like to know something about the people who work with me.'

Of course—how stupid of her to think his interest was personal. A lot of the work he gave her was confidential, he couldn't just reveal those sort of things to anyone. Although James Courtney had never expressed an interest in her private life.

She shrugged. After all, what harm could it do? 'No, I don't have a boy-friend.'

He raised surprised eyebrows. 'You're very attractive.'

With her hair free about her shoulders, and younger, attractive clothing, she was perhaps passable, but she certainly wasn't 'very attractive'.

'When you look the nineteen you are,' he seemed to guess her thoughts. 'And don't try to look and act ten years older.'

Colour flooded Laura's cheeks. 'When did you—I've never—When did you see me looking nineteen?' she asked almost defensively.

He shrugged, a pen held loosely between his long fingers as he played with it idly. Laura found her gaze mesmerised by the way he seemed to almost caress the cold metal, blushing even more as she looked up to find him following her line of vision, his mouth twisting mockingly.

'I can't remember,' he dismissed easily. 'Somewhere.'

She couldn't imagine where, she never appeared anything but the more mature person she was at work. Still, Gideon seemed very certain, and he wasn't a man who would very often be wrong.

'Your mother is a widow, I believe.' He seemed in no hurry to begin dictation; he was completely relaxed, his grey eyes narrowed.

'Yes.' Laura frowned her puzzlement, once again wondering why he needed to know about her private life.

'And you have a brother.'

'Yes,' she nodded. 'He lives in America now.'

'I didn't realise that. He used to work for us, didn't he?'

'Yes,' she acknowledged eagerly. 'It was because he liked working here so much that I—But you don't want to hear about that.' She bit her lip.

'On the contrary,' Gideon prompted.

She shot him a nervous smile; his interest seemed genuine. 'Martin—that's my brother—liked working here——'

'We try to please,' Gideon put in dryly.

'Oh, you do! I mean—Courtneys is a good firm to work for. And——'

'Will you have dinner with me this evening?' he asked quietly.

She raised startled green eyes, her lashes fluttering nervously. 'I—Sorry?' She couldn't have heard him correctly, men like Gideon Maitland didn't ask little nobodies like her out to dinner!

'Dinner. With me. Tonight,' he repeated patiently.

Laura gulped, searching his hard face for some sign of the mockery that never seemed to be far away, but he gazed steadily back at her as he waited for her answer.

But he couldn't really mean it, not *her*.

'Laura?' he prompted at her continued silence.

'I—No. I mean, yes. No——' She was totally confused, the invitation had been totally unexpected.

Gideon gave a tight smile. 'Don't use your mother as an excuse to me,' he more or less confirmed that he had been listening to her conversation for some time before making his presence known. 'I happen to know that your mother is only fifty years old, and that she has more of a social life than you do.'

It was true. Her mother had joined a Widows, Widowers, and Divorcees Club after Laura's father had died, and the friends she had made there were always going out for the evening in a crowd, even on the nights the club didn't meet.

'So?' he prompted again.

'I——' She licked her lips nervously, wondering frantically at the reason for this sudden invitation. Maybe he had argued with Petra Wilde and felt in need of amusement—and she certainly seemed to amuse him. 'You don't mean it.'

'But I do. I never say anything I don't mean.'

'N-never?' she faltered uncertainly.

'Never,' he confirmed.

She swallowed hard. 'You—you really do want to take me out to dinner tonight?'

'I do,' he nodded.

'Why?' Laura frowned.

'Why not?' he gave a tight smile.

'Because——'

'Gideon—Oh,' James Courtney came to a halt just inside the room, looking searchingly at the other man. 'Have you forgotten we have a meeting with Crewe at two-thirty?'

'Not at all,' Gideon denied smoothly. 'Laura and I were just—talking.'

'Indeed?' The older man looked even more puzzled.

Gideon continued to look at Laura, uncaring of his

father-in-law's presence. 'You haven't given me your answer.'

She was aware of James Courtney's speculative looks even if Gideon wasn't, and stood up to leave. 'The answer is no, Mr Maitland,' and she hurried past the surprised James Courtney into her own office.

'Laura!' She hadn't realised Gideon had followed her until he swung her round to face him. 'I'll pick you up at seven-thirty.'

Her embarrassed gaze passed to James Courtney, and then back to Gideon. 'No——'

'Yes!' he insisted firmly, his fingers painful on her arm.

'No . . .' But even she was aware that her denial sounded weak this time. How could he do this to her in front of James Courtney! Wasn't he in the least embarrassed himself in admitting he had invited out his own secretary, a girl far below him both in sophistication and socially? Heavens, one look at Petra Wilde was enough to tell her he must be playing with her—and it was a cruel joke to play on anyone.

'Laura!' Gideon shook her.

'I said no,' she looked away from him, 'And I meant no.'

His hand dropped away from her arm. 'I don't have the time to argue with you now, I'll pick you up at seven-thirty.'

'You——'

'For God's sake give in gracefully, girl,' James Courtney put in tersely. 'Don't you know when you're outmatched?'

She looked at him rebelliously, feeling like a mouse caught between two tormenting cats. 'I don't need any advice from you,' she flashed resentfully. 'As Mr Maitland told me shortly before you arrived, what I do in the evenings is my own affair. And I don't choose to be any rich man's amusement!' She didn't wait to see either James

Courtney or Gideon's reaction to her outburst, but ran out of the office and into the ladies' room further down the corridor. She leant back weakly against the door, hardly able to believe the scene that had just taken place, from Gideon Maitland's dinner invitation to her angry outburst to James Courtney.

Oh God, what had she done! The least she could expect from her outburst would be a verbal or written reprimand, the worst could be instant dismissal. And after her behaviour just now she probably deserved the latter.

She took a deep controlling breath, the ravages of that unpleasant scene on her white shocked face, the eyes staring back at her in the mirror greener than ever. She couldn't stay in here all day, she had to go back to the office, if only to collect her handbag and leave. But she dreaded having to face either of the men again.

Her reflection showed her face to be colourless, her youth showing through in that moment, showing her what Gideon Maitland must have seen, a child dressed up to be a woman.

Well, she didn't work at Courtneys any longer, so the pose of maturity was no longer necessary. She would be just plain Laura Jamieson when she walked out of here, her head held high. The removal of her hair pins was the first move, and she fluffed the auburn waves loose about her shoulders. Undoing the top two buttons of her severely fastened blouse was the next move, folding the collar back over the jacket of her suit. She instantly looked younger, and she felt it too.

Her legs began to shake as she reached her office door. She couldn't hear any explosive voices, but then that didn't mean she wasn't going to be verbally chewed to pieces as soon as she walked in the door. James Courtney could be chillingly polite until he exploded at his victim, and this time she was *it*. She had seen experienced businessmen quake at the thought of a run in with James

Courtney, so what chance did she have of getting out of the building unscathed?

She couldn't believe it—the office was empty! She quickly checked Gideon Maitland's office, just to make sure. Of course, it was almost two-thirty, the two men had an appointment then, and they weren't likely to miss that just for the satisfaction of sacking her personally. No, they would just expect her to go.

She would finish off her work first; she had been halfway through typing a letter. She could leave the completed work on Gideon Maitland's desk—along with her resignation. If they hadn't actually sacked her then she was perfectly within her rights to hand in her resignation. This way she wouldn't have it on her record that she had been sacked.

Her fingers fumbled on the typewriter keys, her eyes opening wide as she looked at the destruction of her letter. It had been quite a lengthy letter too, very technical, and she had prided herself on the fact that she hadn't made a single error, not even on the parts where she didn't understand a word, and now Gideon Maitland had wilfully destroyed her painstaking work. Directly under her neatly laid out letter he had typed 'SEVEN-THIRTY, LAURA'.

She ripped the sheets out of her typewriter, her eyes sparkling with anger. How dared he! How dared he do that to her work? And probably in front of James Courtney too. Well, he could think again, she wouldn't be seeing him at seven-thirty or any other time. And if he wanted this letter retyped then he could damn well do it himself!

Her head was held at an angry angle as she went down in the lift, sparing not a glance for the young receptionist as the other girl shot her a puzzled look.

And no wonder, with this angry sparkle in her eyes, two bright spots of colour in her otherwise pale cheeks.

Laura could never remember losing her temper as much as she had today, the combined arrogance of Gideon Maitland and James Courtney inflaming her in a way that nothing else ever had. And it was an uncomfortable feeling, not in the least pleasant or exhilarating, and she hoped it didn't happen too often in the future.

In the future? What future? She had left her letter of resignation on Gideon Maitland's desk, propped up against the pictures of his wife and little girl. He seemed to spend quite a bit of his time looking at those photographs, so she knew that he wouldn't miss her letter when he got back from his business appointment.

Janice hadn't understated Felicity Maitland's beauty. Laura had been bedazzled by the other woman's flawless features as soon as she saw the photograph, at once seeing why Gideon Maitland and James Courtney missed her so much. Felicity Maitland had looked full of life, a gay teasing smile to her pouting lips, her deep blue eyes laughing with a gaiety that must have been infectious. No wonder Gideon Maitland rarely smiled; when his wife had died she had taken all the laughter out of his life.

And the photograph of his daughter Natalie perhaps explained the reason Janice claimed he had little time for his daughter. Natalie Maitland already showed signs of being as beautiful as her mother had been, her eyes huge and deeply blue, her hair a mass of golden curls.

But for now Laura had to worry about facing her own mother, knowing how furious she would be when she told her she had lost her job—and for such a reason. Her mother would think she was mad for refusing to have dinner with Gideon Maitland—and maybe she was!

'What a day!' Her mother collapsed wearily into a chair, her work at the shop involving being on her feet all day. 'If I have to sell just one more pair of shoes to one more screaming child I swear I'll scream with them!' she sighed.

'Bad as that?' Laura handed her mother a cup of tea.

'Worse,' she grimaced, sipping the refreshing brew gratefully. 'You're home early, love.'

'Yes, well, I——' Now was the time to tell her mother of her resignation. But she couldn't do it! The words just wouldn't come out.

'I wish I could come home early,' her mother groaned, leaning back in the chair. 'Although the way things are going at the shop at the moment I might be home, full stop.'

Laura frowned. 'Business is bad?'

'Well, it isn't good.'

She bit her lip. 'How not good?'

Her mother shrugged. 'Gerry thinks he might have to make redundancies.'

Gerry Blake was the manager of the shoe shop her mother worked in, and if he thought there would be redundancies, then there would be. Oh dear, how could she tell her mother now, the two of them barely managed the flat on two wages, and it would be a tight squeeze to get through until she found another job, but if her mother were to lose her job too . . .!

'How did your day go, love?' Her mother shrugged off her own worry, eager to hear about Laura's day with Gideon Maitland.

'I—It was—interesting,' Laura said lamely.

'Interesting! Is that all?'

No, it had been disastrous! And now she was going to have to try frantically to get herself another job before her mother realised she had lost the one at Courtneys.

Her mother gave her a worried look. 'You didn't upset Mr Maitland in any way, did you?'

She hadn't upset him at all, he had upset her. 'No, of course not,' Laura reassured her.

'Well, how did you get on with him, then?'

'All right,' Laura shrugged. 'Just like a secretary should,
I suppose.'

Her mother shook her head. 'Maybe if you stopped
wearing those clothes and looked like my pretty
Laura . . .'

'Maybe I should,' she agreed, to divert her mother's
attention. 'We could go out on Saturday and look at some
new things.' Although where the money would come from
now that she didn't even have a job she had no idea.

And it didn't seem to have diverted her mother's attention at all. 'So you like Mr Maitland now?' she teased.

She blushed. 'I—He's very attractive.'

'Oh, I'm so glad, Laura,' her mother beamed. 'It never
does any harm to have an influential man like him behind
you.'

'Mother——'

'I know, I know, I'm being pushy. But I want the best
for you, Laura. And there's no reason why Gideon
Maitland shouldn't—like you. Men like him have to
marry someone.'

So her mother had progressed to marriage now! 'He's
already been married, and as far as I know he has no
intention of being so again. He loved his wife very much.
Besides, men like him only have affairs with their secretaries——'

'Don't be such a snob, Laura! You're a very pretty girl,
and——'

Fortunately it was the night for her mother's club, so
she was able to cut short her questioning by reminding
her that she had to get ready to meet her friends.

Her mother certainly had high ideas for her! It had
been impossible to tell her mother she was out of work
when she had such plans for her. Her mother hadn't had
a very easy life, bringing up two children, with her husband away most of the time, and Laura knew she only
meant it for the best when she said she wanted more for

her—but Gideon Maitland was certainly not for her!

She paced restlessly up and down the room once her mother had left, wondering what she was going to do about her jobless state. Jobs weren't so easy to come by nowadays, although secretaries always seemed to be in demand. She would just have to go to an agency tomorrow and hope for the best.

If only she hadn't been antagonised! Turning down Gideon Maitland's invitation wasn't reason enough to sack her, she was perfectly within her rights to do that, but telling her employer to more or less mind his own business was hardly something that could be overlooked, and James Courtney wasn't the most forgiving of men.

When the doorbell rang some time later she was glad of the interruption, her thoughts all worrying ones. It—good heavens! She looked dazedly at the clock on the mantelpiece—seven-thirty exactly!

Gideon Maitland had turned up at seven-thirty as he had said he would!

CHAPTER THREE

LAURA'χ first instinct was not to answer the door. But Gideon knocked again and again, and living in a block of flats as they did, she would be getting complaints from the neighbours if she didn't soon answer the door.

She furiously wrenched the door open, ready to do battle with him, her anger dying in her throat as she saw how handsome he looked in the black fitted shirt and black trousers, the tan jacket tailored to his powerful shoulders and narrow waist. He took her breath away, appearing even more magnificent in the ordinariness of her home. Devastating, that was the word to describe him. He looked devastating.

Laura could only stare at him open-mouthed, not raising any objections when he brushed past her into the flat, closing the door before following him dazedly into the lounge.

'I didn't think you'd be ready to go out to dinner,' he told her, 'so I dressed casually.'

'Yes, I—er—No.' She was doing it again! She took a deep breath, steadying her nervous stuttering. 'Those clothes don't look very casual to me,' she said defensively, knowing that just one of his shirts must cost a fortune, being silk. He probably had them hand-made, as he did the rest of his clothes.

He shrugged dismissively. 'Your mother is out?'

'Yes.'

'Then you may as well have this.' He reached into his breast-pocket, pulling out a white envelope. Her resignation!

She made no move to take the proffered envelope from

46

his strong fingers. 'Mr Courtney——'

'—Liked the way you stood up to him,' Gideon half-smiled.

Her eyes widened. 'He did?'

'Mm,' he nodded. 'James was beginning to wonder whether he'd hired a mouse or a woman as his secretary.'

Considering both men made her feel like the former this wasn't in the last surprising!

'Can I sit down?' Gideon asked mockingly.

Laura flushed at her lack of manners. 'I—er—Yes. Yes, of course. Please do.'

He stretched his legs out in front of him, completely dominating in one of the flower-patterned chairs of their suite. The white envelope containing her resignation was placed on one of the arms of that chair.

Laura eyed it nervously. 'Did you mean it about giving me back my—er—letter?'

He held it out to her once again. 'Here.'

She nervously licked her lips, taking the envelope. 'Oh! You've opened it . . .' she blushed uncomfortably.

'Of course,' Gideon relaxed back in the chair. 'How else would I know it was your resignation? Besides,' he added mockingly, 'it was addressed to me.'

She thrust the envelope in the back pocket of her tight-fitting denims. 'Does Mr Courtney know about it?'

He shook his head. 'There's no reason why he should. This was between us, and that's the way it's going to stay.'

'I just thought——'

Gideon gave an impatient sigh. 'I didn't come here to talk about work, Laura. We can do that in the office to-morrow.'

Her eyes widened hopefully. 'Then I still have a job?'

'Yes.'

A deep sigh of relief left her tensed body. 'I—Thank

you,' she gave him a grateful smile.

He nodded tersely, impatience etched into each handsome feature. 'Perhaps we could talk about us now?' he said dryly.

She gulped. 'Us?'

'Yes, you and me. Or have I misunderstood the situation?' He stood up, at once dwarfing Laura, the broadness of his shoulders seeming to fill the room. 'I thought we were attracted to each other—was I wrong, Laura?' His voice was soft, his grey eyes moving caressingly across her flushed features. 'Was I, Laura?'

'No. I mean—not about me. But you——' she broke off, chewing on her bottom lip.

'I?' He quirked one dark eyebrow questioningly.

'Well, you aren't attracted to me,' she dismissed scornfully, mortified that he *had* known of her stupid infatuation for him.

His face darkened, his grey eyes turned glacial. 'Just when did you become such an expert on my feelings?' he snapped tautly.

Her hands clenched nervously together in front of her. 'I—I didn't,' she said painfully. 'I just thought—Well, everyone knows that you and Miss Wilde are——'

Gideon stiffened. 'What do you know about Petra and myself?'

Laura visibly quaked at his haughty anger. 'I—Only what I've been told.'

'Office gossip,' he dismissed scathingly. 'Haven't you learnt yet that it's usually wrong—or out of date?'

She blinked up at him, unnerved by the way he suddenly seemed closer to her, the smell of the aftershave she found so potent now discernable to her. 'You mean you're no longer seeing Miss Wilde?'

'That's right,' he nodded grimly.

'But——' she broke off, chewing on her bottom lip.

'Yes?' He moved even closer, their thighs almost touching now, his hands on her upper arms, his warm breath ruffling her loose auburn waves. 'What now, Laura?' he bent his head, his lips caressing against her throat.

Heat coursed through her body as Gideon continued to hold her, her breath coming in short, telling gasps. 'I saw you—I mean, I saw a picture of you, with Miss Wilde.' He was biting her earlobe now, breathing erotically in her ear. 'In a magazine,' she fought for sanity against the pleasure his lips were arousing, feeling curiously as if she were drowning. 'You were at the premiere of *Gentle Foe*.'

'That was over a month ago.' His lips were moving slowly across her jaw towards her waiting mouth.

It seemed that she had been waiting for this moment since they had first me. But she had never in her wildest dreams thought Gideon could feel the same way about her, that the attraction could be mutual.

'So you and Miss Wilde are finished now?' she persisted.

'Yes,' he ground out. 'For God's sake, Laura! I don't expect to talk about Petra when I'm making love to you.' His eyes glittered down at her.

Making love to her? Was he? Yes, he was! His hand now rested possessively against her breast, feeling the fast beat of her heart for himself, the shattering effect he was having on her. 'I thought—I thought perhaps you loved her.' Talking of the other woman seemed to be the only way she could stop herself letting Gideon make love to her fully here and now, so devastating was his effect on her.

He moved back with a sigh. 'Petra and I have just spent three weeks together in the Bahamas proving that neither of us loved the other.' His gaze ran slowly over her slender curves in the casual clothes. 'Although there's a lot to be said for physical attraction,' he drawled.

So much for her dream that he might come to love her, as she surely loved him! She had heard that sometimes it happened this way, that sometimes a look was all it took to love someone. But Gideon was too cynical to be so easy to love a second time. And she wasn't the type to go in for an affair, no matter how much she loved him.

She pulled out of his arms. 'I—Would you care for a drink? Tea or coffee?'

His mouth twisted mockingly, his eyes hard as he guessed the reason for her withdrawal. 'Do you have any whisky?'

'Um—I—I'm not sure. Wait a minute,' her face brightened. 'I think Mum got some in last Christmas.' She looked at him anxiously. 'Does whisky go off?'

'Not that I'm aware.' He sat down again. 'Doesn't your brother drink?'

She shrugged. 'A little. When he's home. He's been in America for the past two years.'

'I'll risk the whisky.' He made himself comfortable, unbuttoning his jacket and stretching his legs out in front of him. 'What is your brother doing in America?'

Laura smiled. 'As far as we can tell he's changing his women as often as he changes his shirt.'

There was no answering smile from Gideon. 'Is he still in advertising?'

'Yes. I didn't realise you knew him personally.' She found the half bottle of whisky in the back of the cupboard, took out a glass and half filled it with the fiery liquid.

Gideon eyed the glass mockingly. 'I intend walking out of here, not staggering out,' he taunted. 'What would the neighbours think?'

Laura looked down at the liberal amount of whisky she had poured into the glass. She blushed. 'Shall I pour some of it away?'

'I'll leave what I don't want,' he dismissed, taking the glass from her trembling hand.

Oh dear, she felt stupid. She was doing everything wrong, was acting like a gauche schoolgirl. But she wasn't used to entertaining men, especially men of Gideon

Maitland's calibre, in her home.

'You said you knew my brother,' she prompted.

'No, I didn't. I know he worked in our advertising department, but I didn't know him personally. I know Clive Brady was sorry to lose him.'

Laura sat down opposite him, perched on the edge of her seat. 'Martin's always been the same, never able to settle in one place or one job. My father was in the Navy, and I think Martin inherited his wanderlust.'

'But not you?' He watched her over the rim of his glass.

She gave a selfconscious laugh, feeling as if Gideon had placed her under a microscope, and was now determined to know everything about her. 'I don't have the courage,' she admitted honestly.

'But you would like to travel?'

'Wouldn't everyone?' she shrugged.

His mouth twisted. 'I don't particularly enjoy it.'

'That's because you——' she broke off. 'Sorry,' she muttered.

'Because I what?'

Gideon wasn't a man who particularly appreciated half-sentences, and she seemed to have said nothing else since his arrival. Laura's self-disgust deepened. 'You travel mainly on business, and usually alone,' she made herself say.

He eyed her mockingly. 'Are you saying I should take someone with me?'

'No, I didn't mean——'

'Yourself, for example?' he drawled.

'No!'

'Why not, you're my secretary.'

'I—Only temporarily,' she defended indignantly. How dared he imply she had been angling to be taken away with him on business!

Gideon looked at her calmly. 'It could be arranged that you stay with me permanently.'

Once again her temper rose to save her, or damn her, depending on which way she looked at it. She took her resignation out of her back pocket. 'Perhaps you'd better take this back, Mr Maitland,' she said tightly. 'I have no intention of——'

'Of becoming a rich man's amusement,' he finished dryly. 'But you don't amuse me, Laura,' he added hardly.

'Then what—— Would you just take this and go!' She thrust her resignation at him.

His face hardened, his eyes narrowing. 'Don't push it too far, Laura,' he advised softly. 'I just might take you at your word.'

She drew in an angry breath. Damn the man! He must realise how badly she wanted to keep her job. Her hand shook. 'I don't see how I can continue working for you when you believe I'm intent on having an affair with you. Please, take this.' She would rather face her mother's disappointment than be thought no more than just another willing female to occupy Gideon Maitland's bed. She had some pride, and she didn't intend keeping her job by currying favour with this man, not in the way he obviously expected her to, anyway.

'Laura——'

'Please, Gid—Mr Maitland,' she held her arm straight out, waiting for him to take the letter and go.

'Okay, Laura,' he sighed, sitting forward in his seat. 'You win.'

She swallowed hard. 'I—I do?'

'Yes. For the moment we'll forget about you becoming my—secretary. Now, shall we go out and eat?' he asked briskly.

Laura frowned. 'You aren't taking my resignation?'

He sighed. 'If you insist.' He took the envelope, ripping it, and the letter inside, into four pieces. 'Perhaps you could dispose of these?' he held them out to her.

'Yes,' she agreed huskily.

'Do you have any preference in food?'

'Er—English,' she admitted awkwardly.

'Then get your coat. I'm hungry.' He stood up, stretching like a lazy feline—the dangerous kind.

Laura hurried to her bedroom to get her jacket before he changed his mind. After what she had just told him she hadn't thought he would still be interested in taking her anywhere.

'Will we be late?' she asked as he helped her on with the jacket. 'You see, my mother doesn't know I'm going out——'

'Because you didn't intend to,' Gideon said dryly as they walked down the stairs together. 'What time will your mother be home?'

'About eleven-thirty.'

He nodded. 'I'll make sure you're back before then.'

Laura blushed as he held the door to his Jaguar, open sliding into the low seat, glad that she was wearing trousers. In a dress she would probably have shown more thigh than would have been comfortable. But her attire was caual in the extreme, and she couldn't imagine Gideon being able to take her anywhere that he wouldn't find her appearance embarrassing. If only she had taken a few extra minutes to change!

But she needn't have worried in that direction, the restaurant they entered twenty minutes later was the sort of quietly exclusive place where people dressed as they felt, in whatever was comfortable. It was the sort of place newsworthy people could go to relax, knowing that a reporter would never get past the door.

They were shown to a quiet booth at the back of the room, Gideon choosing to sit beside her rather than opposite her as she had expected him to. The bench seat was quite long, but even so Gideon seemed dangerously close, the hard length of his thigh touching hers, the sensuality of his aftershave once more reaching out to her.

She fiddled needlessly with her knife once the waiter had taken their order, requesting the same as Gideon—honeydew melon, steak and salad to follow, not daring to tell him she had already eaten. She could always leave what she couldn't eat, he would probably put her lack of appetite down to nerves.

And she was nervous. Gideon ignored everyone else in the room, as if it meant nothing to him that the woman sitting a short distance from them was the star of a popular television show, that the man a little farther down the room was a famous film director. Nearly everywhere that Laura looked she recognised people, either from newspapers or television. As far as she could tell she was the only one who didn't fit in here!

'Relax.' Gideon's hand came out to cover hers as he turned on the seat, his leg pressing even harder against hers, his full attention on her flushed features. He frowned. 'You don't like it here?'

'It—I—No,' she admitted huskily.

'Then we'll go——'

'No!' She put her hand pleadingly on his arm. 'Have your dinner. Please.'

'But if you don't like it here . . .'

'I just felt uncomfortable for a moment.' She gave a bright smile. 'I'm all right now.'

'Sure?'

'Yes,' she nodded enthusiastically.

His hand covered hers as it rested on his arm. 'You have no need to feel uncomfortable, Laura. You have as much right to be here as anyone else.'

She wished she could believe him, but she still couldn't relax. Although the sensuous way his fingers played with hers took her mind off the surroundings somewhat.

No one at work would believe that she had actually been out to dinner with Gideon Maitland. Not that she intended telling anyone! But she could hardly believe this herself. Janice had said Gideon was never interested in office girls, so she knew this was a first for him. He had to like her, he had to!

Gideon had necessarily to release her hand when their first course arrived, although he talked warmly to her as they ate their meal. Laura felt cocooned in his warmth, could believe he really cared for her for these few brief hours.

'That wasn't so bad, was it?' he asked lightly as they drove back to her home.

'It was lovely.' And once her initial shyness had passed it had been very enjoyable, she and Gideon seeming to talk about every subject under the sun. She found that Gideon had a lively mind even out of work, his interests very varied.

'We must do it again.'

'Er—yes.' He didn't want to see her again! It was the usual polite comment when you weren't going to be invited out again. How many times had she been told in the past 'we must do this again' and had never heard from the boy again!

'Tomorrow?'

She gasped. 'Tomorrow?'

'Yes,' Gideon smiled, although Laura noticed that these smiles rarely reached the coldness of his eyes. 'Will you have dinner with me tomorrow?'

'I'd love to!'

As she lay awake in bed later that night she wondered why he hadn't kissed her goodnight. He hadn't been so reticent earlier on in the evening, and yet perhaps his courteous goodnight had been proof that he didn't intend mentioning again his first assumption that she would become his mistress.

Well, it might have been courteous of him, but she felt a sense of disappointment, the ache in her body telling her that she had longed for the touch of his lips on hers.

All the time he had been touching her earlier his lips had never once touched hers, and she had been wondering all through the meal how she would react when he did kiss her. Her sense of anticlimax was immense.

It was the early hours of the morning before she finally slept, the deep unfamiliar ache in her body causing her to toss and turn in a restless slumber.

Gideon's attitude was brusque towards her the next day, so much so that she knew their business and personal relationships were to be kept strictly separate. In a way she preferred it that way, although it was hard to believe the stern, decisive man she worked with all day was also the sensually exciting man she was anticipating meeting that evening. Until James Courtney came into her office, that was, the only other person to know of her meeting with Gideon the previous evening.

'Good afternoon, Laura,' he greeted her jovially.

'Mr Courtney,' she returned stiffly, not trusting his mood of friendliness.

He roared with laughter, at once looking younger. 'Still in a temper, are you?'

'Certainly not,' she replied haughtily.

He looked her over without trying to appear as if he were doing anything else. 'Well, at least Gideon's made you look a little more human. I can't abide prim women myself.'

Laura had kept to her decision to be herself, her hair loose about her shoulders, her make-up light but attractive, the severe jacket to her black suit left at home, the rust blouse she wore totally feminine. She flushed her resentment at this man's criticism. 'No one asked you to,' she snapped, forgetting to be repentant to this man.

James Courtney's smile didn't even waver. 'I like you, Laura. You've got spirit!'

So Gideon had been telling the truth, James Courtney had liked the way she stood up to him yesterday. Well, she didn't intend making a habit of it, but nevertheless this man seemed to bring out the worst in her.

'If I were a little younger I'd ask you out myself,' he added tauntingly.

'If you were a little younger you wouldn't need to,' Laura retorted.

'I wouldn't?' He raised one eyebrow.

'You wouldn't be so cantankerous,' she told him bravely. 'And some woman would have snapped you up long ago.'

This time his laughter was even louder. 'I've a good mind to ask you out anyway,' he chuckled. 'You would certainly brighten up my evenings.'

'I might have something to say about that!' Gideon came through from his office, his arm going about Laura's shoulders.

She wasn't sure she liked this display of intimacy in front of his father-in-law, and yet James Courtney didn't seem in the least perturbed.

'You would?' he asked Gideon now.

Gideon looked down at Laura. 'I think so,' he nodded.

'You talked her round last night, then?'

Laura's mouth set rebelliously. 'I don't like being talked about as if I'm not in the room,' she said tartly, shrugging out of the arc of Gideon's arm. 'If you have to discuss me please go through to the other office.'

'How on earth did you survive the evening, Gideon?' James Courtney mocked her display of anger.

'I managed,' Gideon drawled.

'I'm sure you did,' the other man chuckled. 'I could do with an older version of this young lady to put some zest into my own life!'

'Laura's mother is a widow,' Gideon told him.

'Really?' the other man's interest quickened. 'Is your mother anything like you, Laura?'

Her eyes sparkled deeply green as she glared at him.

She wouldn't let this man anywhere near her poor un-
suspecting mother. 'If you mean does she know how to
stand up for herself in the face of rudeness, then the answer
is yes!'

'Perhaps you could introduce me to her some time?'

'I——'

'I don't think Laura's reply is very polite,' Gideon cut
in firmly. 'Was it?' he smiled.

'Perhaps not,' she admitted grudgingly.

'Let's go through to my office, James,' he suggested.
'You seem to bring out the worst in Laura.'

'You've done the opposite, son. She looks quite beautiful,' James Courtney could be heard saying as Gideon closed
the door.

Rude, insufferable man! Would she introduce him to
her mother, indeed! She wouldn't introduce her least
favourite aunt to him. He was——

'Not again, Laura,' Gideon's voice over the intercom
interrupted her furious thoughts.

She had no intention of handing in her notice a second
time. James Courtney had been equally rude to her. He
deserved exactly what he got.

'Laura?'

'Yes, sir,' she assured him that she wasn't going anywhere.

She could hear James Courtney's laughter even through
the thickness of the door. Hateful man!

Over the next few days Gideon treated her with cool politeness. Even when they met in the evenings they talked
only of general subjects, and Gideon made no effort to kiss
or touch her. The nearest they came to intimacy was when
Gideon occasionally put his arm about her waist to guide
her to a seat or help her into his car.

And it was driving her mad! She *wanted* him to kiss her,
and it seemed the more she wanted him to the less likeli-

hood there was of him ever doing so. He always arranged to see her again, was always courteous to her during the day, and yet their evenings always ended with a polite goodnight. If he didn't kiss her soon she knew she was going to make a fool of herself yet again and end up pleading for his kisses.

By the time Friday afternoon came she was in such a state of nerves she jumped every time the door opened or the telephone rang. And it didn't help to know how much her mother expected of her from this friendship. She hadn't particularly wanted her mother to know about her evenings with Gideon, but as each day passed and he continued to ask her out she had to tell her mother who she was meeting. Her embarrassment had been acute on the one evening Gideon and her mother had met; her mother's attitude had been awed to say the least. Laura knew how she felt!

She was seeing Gideon again tonight, although he had made no mention of where they were going for the evening. He always seemed to have something for them to do, evenings at the theatre or ballet, although how he got tickets for these at such short notice she didn't know. She had the suspicion that he had intended going with someone else, Petra Wilde perhaps.

At least James Courtney's tormenting had stopped for a while, as the other man had been in the north of England on business for the last two days. And he wasn't expected back for several more days, much to her delight.

When the telephone rang for about the twentieth time that afternoon she hastily picked up the receiver. 'Gideon Maitland's office, his secretary speaking,' she said automatically.

'Nigel Jennings,' came the cheery reply. 'How are you, Laura?'

'I'm well, thank you. I'm afraid Gid—Mr Maitland isn't here this afternoon, and I'm not expecting him back.'

She had almost slipped up and called him by his first
name!

'Good,' she could hear the smile in Nigel's voice. 'I'll
be up in five minutes.'

'Oh, but—Nigel!' He had rung off!

She slowly replaced the receiver. What on earth could
Nigel Jennings want to see her for?

He arrived well within the five minutes only having
come up from the floor below. 'I had to come and see for
myself,' he perched himself on the edge of Laura's desk.
'And I'm glad to say no one exaggerated.'

She frowned. 'No one exaggerated about what?'

'The vision of loveliness that is now Laura Jamieson,'
he grinned down at her.

Laura blushed fiery red. 'Flatterer!'

'It's the truth. You look lovely. The whole company is
speculating about the change. Most of the women think
you're in love, but us men know that you've suddenly
realised how fascinating we all are.'

She gave him a light laugh, accepting his compliment
for what it was. 'It's definitely the latter,' she teased,
knowing that the chocolate brown dress did suit her, the
square neckline just hinting at the swell of her breasts, its
style shaped to her slender curves. But she was nowhere
near being lovely, in fact, she often wondered what
Gideon saw in her.

'I knew it,' Nigel grinned. 'Now about the firm's do
next week——'

'Is it still on?' She hadn't heard one way or the other,
not that she had been taking a lot of notice of anything this
last week, completely enrapt in Gideon and her growing
love for him.

'It's still on,' Nigel nodded. 'And I was wondering if
you'd go with me?' He looked at her hopefully.

She bit her lip, not knowing what to say. 'Well, I—
I——'

'You have to go, Laura,' he urged eagerly.

'I——'

'Laura is going,' Gideon spoke from behind them. 'With me,' he added pointedly.

Laura hadn't been expecting him back this afternoon, his appearance coming as something of a surprise to her. As did his statement that she was to accompany him to the firm's dinner dance. He hadn't so much as mentioned it to her! Rebellion surged within her at his arrogant assumption that she would be going with him.

Nigel stood up awkwardly, frowning his puzzlement. 'I'd be quite happy to take Laura, Gideon.'

'I'm sure you would,' the other man drawled, completely at ease as he strolled further into the room, his grey pinstriped suit very formal. 'But I'm not taking Laura out of duty, I'm taking her because I want to.'

Laura gasped at the easy way he claimed familiarity with her. And he hadn't so much as kissed her yet!

Nigel looked taken aback. As well he might! 'I—I see. I didn't realise—I mean—God, what *do* I mean!' he groaned his embarrassment.

'When you've worked it out, Nigel,' Gideon said tautly, 'perhaps you could get back to work.' He closed the door behind him as he went into his own office.

Laura was white with anger by this time, Gideon had infuriated her as much as James Courtney did in that moment. Two bright spots of angry colour appeared in her otherwise pale cheeks. 'If the invitation is still open, Nigel——'

He blew through his teeth. 'I don't think it had better be. Gideon—er—made himself very clear.' He was eyeing her warily.

She felt as if she had suddenly turned into public enemy number one. No doubt that was the way it looked to Nigel, Gideon had gone out of his way to make the situation between them clear to him. 'He may have done,' she said stiltedly. 'But did you hear me agreeing with him?'

'No . . .' he acknowledged slowly. 'Hey, look, Laura, if the two of you have had an argument I'd just as soon not be caught in the middle of it, okay?'

He was right, she was't being fair to him to involve him. And she and Gideon hadn't had an argument yet, but she had the feeling they were going to in the very near future. She forced a strained smile to her lips. 'Thanks for the invitation, Nigel, but I doubt I'll even go.'

He gave her a sceptical look, sighing heavily. 'If I'd known about you and——'

'There's nothing to know,' she told him brightly. 'I'd simply forgotten that Gid—Mr Maitland had offered to take me—if I decide to go.' Oh lord, keep your mouth shut, Laura! She was just making matters worse with her fumbling excuses.

Nigel shrugged, obviously crossing her off his list of available women—in future she would be very *un*available as far as he was concerned, she could tell that from his expression. 'I think I'll take Gideon's advice and get back to work.' He stopped at the door, looking back at her. 'And just for the record, Laura, I think you're too good for him.'

She couldn't stop the blush that came to her cheeks as Nigel left the room. He hadn't been fooled for a moment by her halting explanation, and he had probably seen more into the relationship between Gideon and herself than she personally knew there to be. And Gideon had gone a long way to nurturing that impression, damn him!

She didn't even knock before entering his office, her words halting in her throat as she saw he was on the telephone.

He glared at her while still talking to the person on his

private line. 'Yes. Yes, I know you do. Look, I'm not alone,' he said tautly, turning his back on Laura. 'A week or so.' He seemed to listen for several minutes. 'Look, this isn't going to do any good. Petra, for God's sake!' He was deeply angry now.

Laura gulped. He was talking to Petra Wilde! So he was still seeing the other woman after all! She turned and left his office, her face chalky white as she sat down dazedly at her desk. Gideon had told her it was all over between himself and the beautiful actress, and yet he was in his office talking to her now.

He had deceived her. But why? What possible reason could he have for doing such a thing? Had he secretly been laughing at her after all, simply amusing himself with her while Petra Wilde wasn't available?

She felt so stupid, so humiliated! She buried her face in her hands. The whole company would know about her and Gideon by tomorrow, and they would all be expecting her to arrive at the company dinner with him. How could he do this to her? How could he!

'Come into my office for a moment, please, Laura,' he requested quietly from behind her.

She turned, blinking back the tears. 'I—I have a lot of work to do. I——'

'Now, Laura,' he insisted gently, opening the door wider for her to enter.

She must look awful, she knew that. Her nose always went red when she cried, her cheeks blotchy, and the mascara she had put on this morning probably wasn't waterproof and had streaked down her face.

Nevertheless, she passed him with her head held high, jumping slightly as he grasped her arm, preventing her from sitting down, turning her to face him, his eyes narrowed as he studied her face, the door to the outer office firmly closed.

'Why the tears, Laura?' he asked huskily.

Her breath caught in a cross between a hiccup and a sob. 'I'm not crying,' she denied heatedly, staring fixedly at the top button of his waistcoat.

'You look as if you are to me. Was it because of what I told Nigel?' His voice was gentle.

'That, and——and——You were talking to Petra Wilde!' Laura raised her eyes, only to lower them again as she realised just how close he was to her. So close, so very close. And yet not close enough, she knew achingly.

He gave a throaty laugh. 'Are you jealous, Laura?' he teased, holding her firmly in front of him by his hands on her upper arms.

'Yes! I mean, no——I don't know,' she said lamely.

'You have no reason to feel jealous of Petra,' he dismissed the other woman as if she had never existed in his life. 'She'd just heard from a friend of hers that I'm now escorting a very attractive redhead about town,' he teased. 'And she didn't like it. As for Nigel——well, aren't I allowed to feel a little jealousy myself?'

Laura blinked up at him dazedly. 'You, jealous? Of Nigel?'

'Why not?' Gideon pulled her closer, their thighs moulded together in intimacy. 'It seems to me that every time I walk into the office lately I trip over him.'

'Only twice,' she giggled, feeling suddenly wonderfully happy.

'Twice too often,' he growled.

'You were very arrogant, you know.' His closeness was working that familiar magic that she found so disturbing. 'You hadn't even mentioned taking me to the company dinner.'

'Who else would you go with but me?' Once again he was arrogant.

'I wasn't going at all,' she complained.

'Well, you are now, and with me.'

'Gideon——'

'Laura,' he mocked, his head bending as his lips claimed hers.

All thought of Petra Wilde and Nigel fled her mind at the sensuous touch of Gideon's mouth on hers, and she leaned weakly against him as he bent her back over his arm, his lips moving caressingly over hers.

The kiss was everything she had ever thought kissing Gideon would be—and she shivered with uncontrollable delight as his mouth moved sensuously over hers. Her pulse raced, her senses swam as she clung weakly to his broad shoulders, her feet amost off the ground as Gideon held her fiercely against him.

'Well?' he pulled back to breathe raggedly.

Her lips still vibrated and throbbed from his savage possession of them. 'I—I'll come to the company dinner with you,' she told him huskily.

CHAPTER FOUR

GIDEON put her firmly away from him, pushing back the dark hair that had fallen forward over his brow as he kissed her. 'That's decided, then,' he smiled.

Laura instantly reacted to his smile, and melted. 'Yes,' she agreed breathlessly.

He nodded, moving to sit behind his desk, once more the haughty businessman. 'Now about tonight——'

Her gaze sharpened. 'What about it?'

Gideon sighed. 'Our date is off, I'm afraid. Don't look like that,' he said at her disappointed expression. 'I'm no happier about it than you are, but I have to have dinner with a client this evening.'

'Oh.'

'Yes. Gerry Bernstein is over from the States.'

Laura had vaguely heard of him. 'He's very important,' she nodded.

'Yes. I wouldn't normally be the one to entertain him, but with James away . . .' Gideon shrugged.

'I understand,' she gave a bright smile. 'Will I see you tomorrow?' Oh dear, she sounded pushy! But after the way he had just kissed her she didn't think she could bear it if she wasn't to be alone with him again, and soon—and preferably away from the office, somewhere where they could be uninterrupted.

'Not in the afternoon,' he frowned. 'Tomorrow is Natalie's nanny's day off. James usually takes her out on Saturdays, but as he is not expected back until Sunday . . .'

'But couldn't I——' She broke off, biting her lip.

'Yes?' Gideon looked up at her with narrowed grey eyes.

'I was going to suggest I come with you and Natalie,' she gave a nervous laugh. 'It was a stupid idea.'

'You like children?' he rasped.

'Doesn't everyone?' she shrugged.

'No,' he said tautly. 'But you do?'

'I—Yes,' she nodded. Could it possibly be that Felicity Maitland hadn't liked children? She was certainly getting that impression. And if that were so it could be yet another reason why Gideon seemed to resent the little girl. How awful to lose the woman he loved when she was giving birth to a baby she didn't even want.

Gideon shrugged. 'Then by all means come out with us. Natalie usually likes to go to the Zoo. She likes animals,' he explained tersely. 'She just isn't old enough yet to realise the cruelty of shutting them up in those places.'

'She'll learn.' She could hardly believe it, Gideon was actually going to take her out on a threesome with his daughter! She was already looking forward to meeting the little girl.

Gideon frowned at her, his elbows resting on his desk, his fingers placed together in front of him in a pyramid. 'Does it bother you that I have a daughter?'

'Not at all,' she reassured him hastily. 'Did you think it would?'

'It bothers some women.'

Petra Wilde, for example? She must stop feeling jealous of the other woman. It was soul-destroying, and couldn't possibly do her own relationship with Gideon any good. If only Petra Wilde weren't so beautiful! All the women in Gideon's life had been beautiful, especially his wife, and she couldn't be jealous of all of them.

'But not you?' he persisted on the subject of his daughter.

'Not me,' she gave him a bright smile.

He nodded. 'Then I'll call for you tomorrow afternoon and we can all go to Regent's Park Zoo. You'd better go home now, Laura, it's after five.'

'Oh. I—Yes. I'll see you tomorrow, then?' She hesitated at the door, wanting him to kiss her again.

He made no move to do so. 'About two,' he nodded, already engrossed in some papers she had left on his desk. 'You might as well come back to dinner with us too,' he added absently.

'Yes, Gideon.' Laura went back to her own office surrounded by a contented glow, hugging the anticipation of tomorrow to her. Not only was she going to meet his daughter, he was going to take her back to his home too!

The state of excitement she seemed to exist in lately made her wonder how she had ever survived before Gideon came into her life. Her life must have been deadly dull before then.

'Sounds serious,' her mother commented when told of the proposed meeting with Natalie. 'Is it?'

The two of them had had dinner and were now spending a quiet evening together for the first time in a week. It was a pleasant change. Laura hadn't realised how close she was to her mother, more so probably because of Martin's departure.

'On my side, yes,' she admitted. 'But with Gideon it's hard to tell.' He was still so much of an enigma to her. Oh, he could be a charming companion, but underneath the charm she could still detect the harshness she had first noticed about him. He was undoubtedly a complex man, and only people he allowed the privilege would be able to unravel those complexities. No matter how close they seemed to have become in this one short week she knew Gideon hadn't allowed her to see the inner man, the man few people knew.

'Mm,' her mother frowned. 'He's an odd type. I can't work him out at all. He doesn't seem to want an affair with you——'

'Mother!' Laura warned.

'Well, I'm only stating a fact, dear. Unless he's just

working up to the idea slowly? Still, he wouldn't need to introduce you to his daughter if that were the case. Do you think he could possibly be in love with you?'

Laura remembered the intimacy of Gideon's kiss that afternoon, his gentle teasing of her, his admission of jealousy over Nigel Jennings. But love? No, she didn't think so.

'Maybe I'm just a novelty,' she shrugged. 'After all, I'm not his usual type, am I?'

'Men like Gideon Maitland don't have a type, dear,' his mother dismissed. 'I just hope you don't get hurt.'

Laura smiled. 'I thought you said an affair with Gideon was just what I needed to boost my career?'

'I don't think I quite said that, Laura. And I find I don't want that for you, not for my daughter. I'm sure that's how some women get ahead, but after meeting your Gideon Maitland the other night I don't think he's the sort of man I would like you to be involved with. He's very hard. And he wears a mask over his true feelings. I imagine he has a terrible temper.'

She frowned. 'Not that I know of. I don't think I've ever seen him lose his temper.'

Her mother repressed a shiver. 'That's the worst kind. It seethes below the surface, festering and growing. I——'

'Mum!' Laura laughed. 'That's doesn't sound like Gideon at all.'

'No,' her mother sighed, 'perhaps not. If you're going out with him and his daughter tomorrow does that mean your shopping spree is off?'

She had forgotten all about the impetuous suggestion she had made when she thought she had lost her job. 'We can go in the morning.' It would be nice to wear something new when she went out with Gideon in the afternoon. 'He isn't picking me up until two o'clock.'

In the end she bought much more than she could really

afford, three pretty flowered skirts and half a dozen blouses that could be worn with any of the skirts, as their colours contrasted. She also bought a new dress for the company dinner, an emerald-green silky dress that emphasised her feminine curves, its below-knee length showing a long expanse of her slender legs.

'Now what do we do about your hair?' Her mother looked at her critically once they were back out on the street, laden down with their expensive purchases.

Laura frowned. 'There nothing wrong with my hair.'

'It needs styling,' her mother insisted. 'It's a beautiful colour, and all those natural waves should be styled properly. It will be my treat,' she added as Laura went to protest. 'Now that I know I'm not going to be made redundant I can afford to be generous.' Two of her fellow workers had been given notice, but she had managed to keep her job.

In the end Laura had to give in, as her mother had found a hairdresser that could fit her in immediately. She had to admit that the finished result was worth it. Instead of falling in disordered waves to her shoulders her hair had been cut in layers and feathered to a shorter style, framing her face in wispy tendrils, adding depth to her cheekbones, emphasising the colour and size of her eyes until they seemed to dominate her face, like huge jewels.

'I knew I had a beautiful daughter under there somewhere,' her mother smiled her satisfaction as Laura stood ready for her afternoon date with Gideon.

Her mother was right, for once in her life she looked beautiful, and for the first time in her young life she actually *felt* beautiful. The green and black flower-print skirt swung about her slender legs, her ankles narrow and shapely in the black sandals she wore, the black blouse tucked neatly into the narrow waistband of the skirt, her make-up light, her hair still in its new easy-to-manage style.

When the Jaguar drew up outside the building, and she heard Gideon's firm tread on the stair, her heart leaped with anticipation of his reaction to her appearance. Would he too think she looked beautiful?

Her mother went to answer the door. 'You stay in your room until I call you,' she instructed. 'You mustn't let him think you're too eager.'

Laura shook her head as her mother bustled out of the room. Gideon must already know how she felt about him, she wasn't exactly an expert at hiding her feelings. She left that to him.

After several minutes, when her mother still hadn't called her, she decided she had better go out anyway. She soon discovered the reason for her mother's omission. She was holding Natalie Maitland in her arms, completely enraptured by the child.

The photograph on Gideon's desk was a little out of date, the child her mother was holding was no longer the baby she had looked then, but was now an adorable little girl. The pretty pink dress and matching pinafore suited her blonde cuteness, her teeth were very small and white as she chuckled at Laura's mother. She was a beautiful child, turning with interest as she sensed Laura's presence in the room. Huge blue eyes dominated her dimply face, the lashes long and silky.

Her own appearance forgotten, Laura moved towards her mother and the toddler. 'Oh, Gideon, she's beautiful!' She tentatively touched the dimply fingers that reached out to her.

He had stood up as soon as she entered the room, more casually dressed than she had ever seen him, although the denims and black silk shirt were of the finest quality. But nevertheless he looked more ruggedly handsome than she had ever seen him, the denims old and faded, fitting low down on his hips, held in place by a thick black leather belt. It hadn't occurred to her that Gideon would bring

Natalie up to the flat, but as he was driving them himself he could hardly leave the little girl downstairs in the car. Natalie was certainly a hit with her mother, the two of them were chuckling together.

Laura let go of the little girl's hand, turning to Gideon. 'She's adorable,' she told him huskily.

'So are you,' he said. 'You've changed your hair,' he frowned.

She looked at him uncertainly, unsure whether his words were critical or complimentary. What if he didn't like it . . . 'Yes,' she acknowledged with reluctance.

Gideon smiled. 'I like it.'

'You do?' she sighed with relief.

'It's very pretty,' he nodded. 'Now, shall we get Natalie and be on our way?' he suggested.

'I—Yes. Mum?' She put her arms out for the little girl, experiencing a thrill of pleasure as Natalie didn't even hesitate, her dimply arms clinging about Laura's neck.

'You must bring your daughter to see us again,' Laura's mother told him. 'She really is lovely.'

'Yes,' he nodded abruptly. 'If you're ready to go, Laura?'

Her mother raised her eyebrows at Gideon's brusque behaviour, but Laura just shrugged it off. She knew what had caused his terseness. Over the next couple of hours she discovered that Gideon loved his daughter with a reluctance that the baby was too young to realise yet. His manner was offhand to say the least, his only show of emotion to her coming when Natalie slipped and fell, scraping one of her knees enough to make her cry.

Gideon scooped her up into his arms, inspecting the slightly bleeding knee. 'You should have been watching her more closely,' he turned on Laura. 'It was your idea to let her run around on her own. You should have watched her,' he accused.

Laura didn't think now was the right time to point out

that it had been his decision to let Natalie toddle around. The Zoo was completely enclosed, so she couldn't come to any serious harm. And she had been watching the little girl, she just hadn't been quick enough to catch her when she tripped. Much as she knew Gideon would deny it, he was reacting like any other worried parent would when their child hurt itself, blaming everyone else but himself.

'Let me take her to the washrooms and get her cleaned up,' she offered soothingly. 'I think I have some plasters in my bag.'

Natalie stopped crying as soon as they entered the washroom, while Gideon prowled about outside. 'You little fraud!' Laura laughed as the little girl beamed at her. 'So you just wanted Daddy to make a fuss of you, did you?' Maybe Natalie did sense her father's reservation towards her after all, she had heard that children could sense things when adults couldn't. 'Your daddy loves you,' she assured her as she cleaned up the knee, discovering that only one of the scratches was big enough to bleed, and even that had stopped now. It certainly didn't seem to bother Natalie any more, although she looked down interestedly as Laura applied the plaster.

'Bad,' she announced proudly.

She looked so cute in that moment, her little chin jutting out determinedly, her face full of charm, that Laura knew a wealth of love for the little girl. How easy it would be to love this toddler almost as much as she loved the father.

Gideon stopped his pacing as they rejoined him, sparing only a cursory glance for his daughter, his grey-eyed gaze fixed on Laura's glowing face. 'I'm sorry,' he muttered.

'It doesn't matter,' she dismissed, unable to look at him, an apology was the last thing she had been expecting. 'Show Daddy your knee, Natalie.'

'Bad,' the little girl announced again.

'It's better now, Natalie,' her father smiled, once again

turning to Laura. 'I'm afraid I'm the one who was bad. I didn't mean to shout at you, Laura,' he repeated his apology.

Delicate colour tinged her cheeks. 'I told you, it doesn't matter. I think Natalie might like something to eat now,' she suggested.

'Cake,' Natalie put in hopefully.

Both adults laughed. Gideon's arm went about Laura's shoulders as she carried his daughter. 'I'll have to re-member in future that she understands what I say to you,' his tone implied that some of the things he said wouldn't be suitable for young ears.

Laura glowed with the implication that there would be a future for them, not caring at all when Natalie spilt some of her orange juice down her new skirt.

'She's a little free with her food and drink,' Gideon bent to mop up the excess fluid. 'I'm sorry about this——' he had looked up, their gazes locking and holding, and Laura trembled from the warmth of his hand on her thigh. 'Let's get out of here,' Gideon muttered. 'I want to be alone with you.'

Laura flushed, wanting to be alone with him too. A sudden awareness had sprung up between them, an awareness that needed to be assuaged.

Natalie chose that moment to start throwing cake on the ground, chortling her delight.

'Oh no, you don't, young lady!' Laura removed the plate from out of harm's way, wiping the baby clean with a napkin. 'Time to leave, I think,' she smiled at Gideon, the little girl having been forgotten during that brief moment of awareness.

'Later?' he prompted huskily. 'When Natalie has gone to bed?'

'I—Yes, later.' She couldn't meet the warmth of his gaze, his eyes no longer the cold, hard grey she had become accustomed to.

The tension between them was broken when Natalie pointed to the wolves and exclaimed 'Doggy!' in a loud voice. Several passersby joined in their amusement.

'You'll have to tell her about wolves once she's older,' Laura laughed.

'Did your mother ever tell you about them?' Gideon asked softly.

She looked up at him sharply. 'She mentioned that it never pays to get too close to one,' she said slowly.

He nodded, unlocking the car door for her. 'Does she know about Nigel Jennings?'

Nigel? He had been talking about *Nigel*? 'There's nothing to know,' she dismissed easily.

'Nothing?'

'No,' she said tightly. 'What is this, Gideon, an inquisition?'

He shrugged. 'I just wondered if you'd ever been out with him.'

'Not yet,' she replied tautly, their camaraderie completely gone now.

Gideon's expression tightened. 'By that I take it you're thinking about it?'

'I could be,' she nodded.

'And if I asked you not to?'

'Do you have that right?'

'No,' he ground out. 'There was a lot to be said for the Victorian era,' he snapped. 'At least women knew their place in those days.'

'Below stairs? Helping keep the master's bed warm? Or having so many children they usually died twenty years too early?' Bright spots of angry colour had appeared in her rebellious face. 'I suppose that would have appealed to your machismo. Just think, Gideon,' she scorned. 'If this were a hundred years ago, as my employer you would be able to order me to go to bed with you.'

'The idea of forced sex has never appealed to me,' he

said tightly, his face white beneath his tan, his eyes a cold, metallic grey.

'You surprise me,' she snapped, beyond being polite, her anger fiery hot.

The look he shot her spoke volumes. Laura turned away, staring fixedly out of her side window. What on earth was she *doing*, arguing with Gideon just because he had dared to question her about Nigel Jennings? It was a stupid, senseless quarrel, and she was aware that she could have alienated Gideon for ever.

She quite expected him to take her straight to her home, but instead he drove to Hampstead. His home was as she had expected it to be, a veritable mansion run by an army of servants. The inside was tastefully decorated and furnished, seeming to have a woman's touch, even though there was no longer a mistress of the house, giving Laura the impression that Felicity Maitland had had a hand in the gracious beauty of this house before she died.

Laura felt lost amongst its opulence; the servants made her feel uncomfortable, Gideon's air of command instantly taking him even farther away from her.

'Sit down, won't you,' he invited distantly. 'I'll just get Jane to take Natalie up for her bath.'

Laura would like to have offered to do that, but she knew her offer wouldn't be appreciated. Gideon looked very forbidding. She wanted to offer even more when it seemed Natalie didn't want to leave her, her little arms clinging about her neck.

Gideon pried the clinging fingers loose and handed the now screaming child to the young girl who had come at his summons.

'Dinner should be ready in about an hour,' he told Laura stiltedly.

She bit her bottom lip. 'Do you still want me to stay?'

He looked at her coldly. 'Do you want to?'

'Yes.'

'Then stay,' he shrugged dismissively. 'Would you care for a drink?' He moved to the array of drinks on the sideboard. 'I know it's only six-thirty, but I feel in need of one,' his mouth twisted.

'No, thank you, not for me.' Laura watched as he poured himself a drink and drank it down in one gulp, refilling his glass to sit down in the chair opposite her. 'Gideon ... I'm sorry,' she said pleadingly, knowing it was up to her to make the first move.

He looked at her coldly. 'Are you?'

'Yes. I—I said some stupid things just now, things I didn't mean.'

'Didn't you?'

'No! I—I'm just not used to being questioned about—about——'

'Your other men,' he drawled insultingly.

Laura flushed. 'I don't have any other men!'

'Don't you?'

'No!' she denied heatedly.

He shrugged. 'If you say so.'

'I do!'

'Then why react the way you did?'

'Because—because I resented your implication. And because since meeting you I've discovered a temper I never knew I had,' she added lightly, wishing the bitterness would go from his eyes. 'Oh, Gideon——' she was prevented from saying anything further by a light knock sounding on the door.

It was Jane. 'Natalie has had her bath and supper, Mr Maitland,' she informed him breathlessly.

He nodded. 'I'll be up in a moment.'

'Yes, sir.' She went out, closing the door behind her, obviously infatuated with her employer.

Gideon stood up in one fluid movement. 'I'm just going up to say goodnight to Natalie,' he told Laura coldly. 'I shouldn't be long.'

She had never felt so miserable in her entire life. That short moment of intimacy at the Zoo might never have happened, from Gideon's attitude to her now.

He came back fifteen minutes later, and she couldn't tell what his reaction was to still finding her here. 'I read Natalie a story,' he revealed abruptly. 'She doesn't understand a word, but she seems to enjoy them.'

'Yes.' Laura's eyes were wide with apprehension. Things seemed to have gone terribly wrong between them today, and she was aware that it was mainly her fault.

'Gid——'

'Lau——You first,' he invited as they both went to speak at once.

She gave a nervy smile. 'I was just going to repeat that I really am sorry.'

'For what?' he asked tersely.

'For—for——'

'You have nothing to apologise for,' Gideon sighed, running a hand through his already tousled dark hair. 'I'm behaving unreasonably——'

'Oh no——'

'Yes,' he insisted. 'It's nothing to do with me who you choose to go out with, either now or in the past.' He was prowling up and down like one of the caged tigers Natalie had found so fascinating that afternoon.

'No . . .' she agreed slowly.

'Just as I don't expect you to question me on my movements in the past.'

He couldn't have told her more clearly how little she meant in his life, and all her fragile dreams of having him come to love her as she loved him fell in broken pieces at her feet. Something of her feelings must have shown in her face, because Gideon moved to sit next to her on the sofa.

'Which isn't to say,' he said huskily, 'that I don't want you to be very interested in my movements now.'

She made herself smile at his teasing tone, not wanting

him to guess how deeply her feelings were already involved with him, how she wanted to know what he did every minute of the day. She was just another woman to him, and would probably be replaced as rapidly as he had put her in Petra Wilde's place.

'Laura?' he questioned sharply.

'I—er—Yes?'

He smiled, not sensing any of her distress. 'It may have escaped your notice,' he drawled, 'but we're very much alone now.'

She blushed as she once again recalled the awareness that had suddenly sprung up between them that afternoon. 'So we are,' she agreed lightly, not wanting to appear too eager.

'What are you going to do if I kiss you?'

Her mouth quirked. 'Kiss you back?'

'I hope so,' he said softly, moving to sit closer to her, one of his hands coming up to gently caress her cheek. 'In one short week you've grown into a beautiful young woman,' he told her thoughtfully. 'I can't understand why you wanted to hide your beauty behind those drab clothes you used to wear for the office.'

'Maybe to keep off the wolves,' she mocked, not even knowing she *was* beautiful.

He gave a husky laugh. 'It didn't work.'

'No. Actually, I did it to give me a look of mature efficiency.'

Gideon nodded. 'It almost worked too.'

'But you have a discerning eye,' she said dryly.

'Very discerning,' he smiled. 'Especially where sexy redheads are concerned.'

Sexy? Was she? 'I'm not a redhead,' she told him to cover up her embarrassment. 'My hair is auburn.'

'It's beautiful. Laura—Oh damn!' he muttered as Jane knocked on the door to announce dinner. 'We get more privacy at the office,' he groaned as they went through to the dining-room.

Laura was in a state of total confusion. Did Gideon want an affair with her after all? It would appear so. And was her answer to be yes or no? She was very much afraid it was going to be yes. Afraid, because she was going to be hurt by such a relationship. But she would be hurt even more if she said no!

'Talking of the office,' Gideon remarked as they ate, 'Diane will be back on Monday morning.'

Laura almost choked over her soup. 'She—she will?'

'Mm,' he nodded. 'She called me yesterday, but I forgot to tell you.'

He had *forgotten* to tell her that she would no longer be working with him! The rest of the meal passed in a haze for her, and the food could have been absolutely awful for all she tasted it, although she doubted it was; Gideon's kitchen would be run as efficiently as the rest of his life was. But she couldn't even have said what she had eaten. On Monday she was to go back to working for James Courtney! If she saw as much of Gideon in the office as she had that first week then she wouldn't see much of him at all.

'You're very quiet,' he said suddenly.

'It's all the fresh air I've had today,' she excused.

'Natalie was exhausted too.'

Her expression instantly softened. 'She's a lovely child.'

Gideon frowned. 'You really mean that, don't you?'

Laura looked taken aback. 'But of course!'

He looked up at the manservant who had been quietly serving them. 'Miss Jamieson and I will take our coffee in the lounge.' He stood up, pulling Laura's chair back for her. 'And we're not to be disturbed,' he added firmly.

'No, sir.' The man stared woodenly in front of him.

Laura flushed deeply red. 'I wish you hadn't done that,' she mumbled once she and Gideon were alone in the lounge. 'He'll think—Your servants will think——'

'Yes?' he sounded amused.

Her eyes sparkled angrily. 'They'll think you intend making love to me,' she snapped.

His hands grasped her shoulders. 'And what makes you think I don't?'

'I—Well—Do you?'

'Not completely,' he laughed mockingly at the confusion in her face. 'Not yet.'

'N-not yet?'

'I never believe in rushing these things.'

'Is that why you haven't kissed me all week?'

His expression mocked. 'Did you want me to?'

'No,' she snapped her resentment. 'No, I didn't! And I don't want you to kiss me now either. You——'

She didn't get any further, for Gideon's mouth on hers effectively stopped her heated flow of words.

She couldn't deny her love for this man, couldn't prevent her instantaneous response to the savagery of his kiss, her senses spinning. He continued to plunder her mouth as she clung to him, his arms like steel bands about her slender body.

Gideon's kiss was fierce in its intent, demanding that she respond fully to him, wanting her full surrender, making Laura almost feel as if she were being submerged into his body.

His lips on her throat were causing wild sensations to course through her, her breathing ragged as his fingers deftly undid the top two buttons of her blouse, his hand splayed out across the creamy swell of her breasts. No man had ever touched her this intimately, his fingers now probing beneath the silky cups of her bra, capturing the already aroused nipple between finger and thumb.

Laura pulled away, her eyes mirroring her shock. 'Please—don't!' she gasped shakily, and twisted out of his grasp, effectively removing the hand that had caused her panic.

'Why?' he demanded harshly.

'I—You hurt me!' she accused desperately.

'Liar!' he rasped, kissing her again, this time allowing her no chance to protest, and the two of them were soon lying side by side on the wide sofa, Gideon dispensing with all the buttons on her blouse, the unfastening of her bra posing no trouble to him either.

He also showed Laura what she should do to please him, unbuttoning his own shirt to push her hands inside against his warm flesh. It was a time of wonder for Laura, the discovery of the beauty and eroticism of a man's body, Gideon's skin firm and muscled beneath her tentative touch.

He raised his head. 'Am I still hurting you?' he mocked her total surrender, his mouth against her breast, her gasps this time having been ones of pleasure.

'No . . .' she groaned, lost in a sea of sensual abandon.

'And am I forcing you?' he added tautly.

She knew he was referring to the insult she had thrown at him earlier, and she blushed guiltily. 'You know you aren't,' she said miserably.

'I didn't think I was,' he said grimly. 'And seeing you aroused appeals to my "machismo" much more than forcing any woman.' He swung his legs to the floor, sitting up to button his shirt. 'Natalie's nanny will be home shortly, I think we should make ourselves presentable.' He stood up to tuck the black shirt into the waistband of his denims.

Laura hastily adjusted her clothing. 'Gideon——'

'You missed a button.' He did it up with impersonal fingers, his calm features showing none of the heated passion they had shared a few minutes ago.

'Gideon?'

'Yes?' He looked at her with guarded eyes.

His coldness made her flinch. 'Nothing. It isn't important.' She turned away, shamed colour flooding her cheeks.

He swung her round to face him, the warmth once more back in his face. 'I'm not the romantic lover you expected, hmm?' he teased lightly.

She blinked back her tears. 'No. I mean—You——'

'Do you love me, Laura?' he queried softly.

Her eyes flew open in dismay. She had given herself away! At some time during their lovemaking she had divulged her love for him!

'Do you?' he persisted.

'No,' she denied heatedly, 'of course I don't. I hardly know you. I——'

Gideon once more kissed her, slowly this time, druggingly, his lips firm and moist as they moved over hers, his tongue moving erotically along her lower lip, his hands slowly caressing the slenderness of her waist and thighs.

'Do you love me, Laura?' he murmured close to her earlobe, biting gently into the soft skin.

'Yes,' she groaned helplessly. 'God, yes!'

'Yes, what?'

'I love you,' she gasped as he traced the outline of her ear with his tongue. 'I love you, Gideon.'

'I——' Suddenly he stiffened. 'I think I just heard Lisa arrive home.' He moved away from her. 'She'll probably come in here in a moment,' he explained.

Laura disliked Lisa Harlow before she even entered the room, sure that if the other woman hadn't returned at that moment that Gideon would have told her of his own love for her.

But when the other woman walked into the room she felt her antagonism deepen. Lisa Harlow was about thirty, very beautiful, her hair a lovely flame red—and she didn't look like anyone's nanny! What had Gideon said about having a discerning eye where sexy redheads were concerned? And this woman lived here in his home with him!

CHAPTER FIVE

'COME in, Lisa,' Gideon invited smoothly as she seemed to hesitate in the doorway.

The woman moved with the grace of a model, the rust-coloured dress she wore showing the perfection of her figure, her height adding to the illusion of flowing grace.

'I didn't realise I was interrupting anything . . .' her voice was husky and attractive, her expensive perfume invading every corner of the room.

Laura felt very young and gauche in the face of the other woman's sophistication, feeling like an interloper instead of a guest as Lisa Harlow looked at her with cold blue eyes. It was almost as if Lisa were the hostess and Laura an uninvited guest she had unwillingly to be polite to.

'You aren't interrupting anything,' Gideon told her warmly. 'Laura and I were only talking.'

Only talking? She had just told him she loved him and he dismissed it as 'only talking'! She felt as if he had physically hit her.

She was only half aware of the introductions being made, the other woman's smile was only as lukewarm as her own. They didn't like each other, that much was obvious from the first.

'Could I have a drink, Gideon?' Lisa sat down, crossing one silky leg over the other, having no intention of leaving the room now that she was here.

'Of course. Laura?' he turned to her.

'No, thank you,' she refused tightly.

Gideon poured out two glasses of whisky, adding water and ice to Lisa's without even bothering to ask, making Laura wonder how often he and the other woman drank together like this in the evenings. Gideon certainly knew her taste in drinks—did he also know her tastes in love-making? He certainly hadn't reached that peak of experience by remaining celibate. Of course, he had been married, but nevertheless . . .

'Mm, just as I like it,' said Lisa after her first sip of the drink, almost as if she knew the resentment of Laura's thoughts. 'Tell me, Laura,' she drawled, 'is Gideon as—thoughtful to work for at the office as he is here?'

Laura drew a steadying breath, looking at Gideon as he leant nonchalantly against the unlit fireplace. Didn't he realise that this woman was baiting her? Obviously not. 'He's very—thoughtful, there too,' she replied with saccharine sweetness. 'Did you have a pleasant day off?' she added to let the other woman know that *she* was the one who had been with Gideon all day, and not her.

'Very nice, thank you. Although I don't really need a day off,' she said warmly. 'Natalie is such a delight to take care of.'

'Isn't she?' Laura agreed sweetly.

'Laura and I took her to the Zoo today,' Gideon explained lightly, still seemingly unaware of the hostility between the two women—or else choosing to ignore it.

Arched eyebrows rose. 'You only had to say, Gideon. You know I appreciate these days off, but they aren't really necessary. I'm sorry your day was ruined, Miss Jamieson.'

'On the contrary, Miss Harlow——'

'*Mrs* Harlow,' the other woman corrected smoothly.

Laura looked startled. 'I didn't realise you were married.'

'Oh, I'm not, not now,' she said unconcernedly. 'I'm just another statistic on the divorce records. I wasn't as lucky as Felicity in my choice of a husband,' she gave Gideon a warm, intimate smile.

Laura swallowed hard. 'You knew—I mean——'

Amused blue eyes returned to her from smiling at Gideon. 'Felicity and I were very good friends,' Lisa informed her triumphantly.

'I see,' Laura bit her lip.

'Do you?' the other woman drawled, sipping her drink.

Laura glanced at Gideon and then back to Lisa. Couldn't Gideon see this woman intended being the next Mrs Gideon Maitland, was telling Laura that any ideas she might have in that direction should be forgotten? She could have told Lisa Harlow that she had nothing to fear from her, her love for Gideon might be admitted, but she had no illusion of where that love would take her.

She stood up. 'I think I should be going now, Gideon.'

'Of course.' He put his glass down on the table, empty now. 'You'll excuse us, Lisa?'

The other woman smiled. 'I have something I want to discuss with you, Gideon, so I'll wait up for you.'

'Fine,' he nodded. 'I'll get your coat, Laura.'

'I only have this cardigan with me,' she told him woodenly.

Gideon looked at her with narrowed grey eyes, seemingly puzzled by her behaviour. 'Then I'll just get my jacket.'

He was displeased with her, she could tell that. Well, what did he expect! Lisa Harlow had as much as stated their intimacy. And that remark about waiting up for him . . .! Not even a simpleton could misunderstand the implication behind that. Although Gideon still seemed to want to take *her* home.

She looked down awkwardly at her hands once she was left alone with the other woman, aware that Lisa Harlow was watching her with narrowed blue eyes.

'I don't intend losing him a second time,' she remarked suddenly.

Laura blinked dazedly at this open attack. 'I—I beg your pardon?' she frowned.

'Fifteen years ago I was stupid enough to throw Gideon over in favour of the ex-Mr Harlow,' Lisa drawled. 'Gideon married Felicity, and I married Charles.'

'You're saying that you and Gideon—that you and he were——'

'Were friends,' Lisa finished pointedly. 'And I intend that we'll be even closer than that now. You don't think I look after Natalie because I need to work, do you? Charles paid me a handsome sum at our divorce. And you have to admit that as far as Gideon is concerned, I have the advantage . . .'

'Because you live here,' Laura reasoned dully.

'Exactly,' the other woman smiled. 'Save yourself a lot of heartache, Laura, and forget about Gideon.'

'You have no right——'

Lisa Harlow's expression was suddenly vicious. 'Don't make me break you up, Laura. I can do it, just like that,' she clicked her fingers. 'And I will, believe me.'

Oh, she believed her, she just couldn't believe this was actually happening. 'Gideon——'

'Wants to go to bed with you,' Lisa drawled. 'Is that what you want, a brief affair?'

'It's none of your——'

'He's a wonderful lover,' the other woman continued, completely composed once again. 'Very accomplished. And I should know.'

'Excuse me,' Laura choked, very pale, 'I—I have to go.'

'Laura——'

'Goodbye, Mrs Harlow.' She wrenched the door open—and bumped straight into Gideon!

'Sorry, I—Hey,' he grasped her upper arms, looking down at her sharply. 'What's wrong?'

'Nothing.' She stared fixedly at the third button down on his shirt. 'I'm ready to leave now.'

'I just want to have a word with Lisa——'

'I think I'll wait outside,' Laura said jerkily. 'I could

do with some air.' The things Lisa Harlow had told her made her feel sick.

'Wait here,' Gideon ordered.

'No——'

'Yes,' he insisted firmly.

She was really too numb to move, following him outside when he rejoined her a few minutes later, his arm going about her shoulders as she began to shiver.

'Please, don't!' She pushed him away from her, feeling close to tears.

He frowned. 'Laura——'

'Would you please take me home!' Her voice was shrill.

'Of course.' Gideon wrenched open the car door, closing it with a slam once she had got inside, joining her within seconds. 'What's the matter?' he sighed after several minutes of silent driving.

'Nothing.' She stared straight in front of her, holding back the tears with effort.

'I don't believe that,' he answered patiently. 'Did Lisa say something to upset you? I know she isn't everyone's favourite person.'

Laura turned accusing green eyes on him. 'Is she yours?'

He frowned. 'What the hell is that supposed to mean?'

She drew a deep breath. 'What do you think it means?'

'You tell me,' Gideon invited grimly.

'Are you and she lovers?' She caught her breath with the enormity of that question.

'No.'

'No?'

'No,' he repeated firmly.

'Oh, I——' she frowned her consternation. 'Were you ever?' she added sharply.

'Years ago,' he nodded. 'Before I married Felicity.'

Laura swallowed hard. 'But not now?'

'No.'

Why had she taken the other woman's word for it? Lisa Harlow was in love with Gideon, that much was obvious, but he had given no indication that he returned that love. If he had wanted to marry the other woman surely he would have done so by now.

But still the doubts persisted. 'She lives in your house——'

'And it naturally follows that I sleep with her?' Gideon rasped.

'Well, no . . . But if you were lovers in the past——'

'Almost fifteen years ago!'

'But——'

'I don't sleep with her, Laura,' he told her coldly. 'You please yourself whether or not you believe that.'

'Oh, I do——'

'Then what the hell are we arguing about? If Lisa gave you a different impression then I'm sorry. But I don't intend explaining my actions to you again.'

'I'm sorry,' she said stiffly, seeing with dismay that they had arrived back at her home. 'I am sorry, Gideon,' she turned to look at him pleadingly.

'Yes,' he acknowledged tersely.

'Will I see you tomorrow?'

'Yes,' he sighed, leaning forward to kiss her lightly on the lips. 'You'd better go inside.'

'I—Yes.'

He gave a casual wave before driving off, telling her better than words that he was still annoyed with her. And no wonder! She had believed every word Lisa Harlow told her, had judged Gideon without question, and he had a right to be angry about that.

It was the ringing of the telephone that woke her the next morning. She groped her way blindly out to the telephone in the lounge, knowing that her mother wouldn't emerge from her bedroom until at least twelve o'clock, not on a Sunday.

'Laura?' came the husky response to her reciting of the telephone number.

Gideon! Heavens, it was only seven-thirty in the morning. 'It's very early,' she told him waspishly.

'I know,' he sighed at her stating of the obvious. 'But I have to leave town urgently for a couple of days. I thought you might want to know,' he added tautly.

'You're going away?' she voiced her dismay, coming awake in a hurry.

'Until Wednesday or Thursday,' Gideon confirmed.

That wasn't a *couple* of days, that was almost a week! 'I see,' she said tightly. 'Well, have a good trip.'

'Is that all you have to say?' he snapped.

What else could she say? She wasn't going to see Gideon for days on end—and it was going to seem like years. 'What else is there?' she asked dully.

'Nothing, obviously. I'm sorry I troubled you.' The telephone was slammed down the other end, so loud it almost split Laura's eardrums.

Now what had she done? At least Gideon had taken the time to call her, and if it was for business then he really couldn't help having to go away. She had to speak to him before he left.

It was just her luck that Lisa Harlow was the one to answer the telephone! 'Gideon is very busy, Laura,' she told her coldly. 'He's going away, and——'

'Yes, I know,' Laura put in quietly.

'You do?'

'Yes.' The other woman was shaken by the knowledge, she could tell that.

'Then couldn't it wait until he gets back?'

'No, it couldn't,' she replied firmly.

'He's upstairs——'

'Mrs Harlow, I want to talk to Gideon,' she repeated patiently.

'Laura——'

'Mrs Harlow!'

'Very well,' Lisa snapped. 'But don't keep him long, he has to fly to Manchester in a few minutes.'

'I'll do my best,' she said sweetly. 'Now if you wouldn't mind . . .'

'Very well,' the other woman answered tightly, 'I'll get him for you.'

Lisa Harlow no longer sounded the assured woman of the night before. She had probably expected her warning to have made more impact than it had, was probably surprised Laura was still in Gideon's life.

'Don't forget you have to leave for the airport in a few minutes,' she could hear Lisa telling Gideon before he came on the line.

'Yes?' he enquired tersely.

'Gideon, I'm sorry about earlier,' she licked her lips nervously, her hand tightly gripping the receiver. 'I wasn't properly awake. I didn't mean to sound offhand.'

He didn't answer for long, painful seconds. 'Are you usually bad-tempered first thing in the morning?' he asked at last.

Laura laughed her relief at his teasing tone. 'Yes.'

'Mm. I'll have to remember that.'

'You—you will?'

'I have a good remedy for it.'

Colour flooded her cheeks at the intimacy of his tone. 'I—You—I——'

He laughed huskily. 'Are you blushing?'

'Er—Yes.'

'I forget how young you are at times. Still love me?' His voice lowered, giving the impression he didn't want their conversation to be overheard.

'Yes,' she answered truthfully.

'I'll try to get back Wednesday or Thursday,' he told her briskly. 'James has hit some snags in Manchester that we weren't expecting. But I'll definitely be back in time to take you to the company dinner on Friday. You won't forget you're going with me?'

As if she could ever forget a date with him! 'I'll look forward to it.'

'So will I. I have to go now, Laura. If you could just spend Monday morning with Diane explaining any work we might have left outstanding, James should be back Tuesday.'

Their goodbyes weren't exactly romantic, but she had Friday to look forward to.

Just as she was about to replace her own telephone receiver she thought she heard another click, as if a second receiver had been replaced in Gideon's house. Lisa Harlow on an extension?

God, she was becoming paranoic about the woman! That second click must have just been static on the line.

She missed Gideon, missed working with him, and missed him in the evenings. But James Courtney returned on Tuesday as Gideon had said he would, and he kept everyone on their toes.

But Gideon didn't telephone her again, and by Thursday evening she was becoming agitated. He had said he would definitely be back in time to accompany her tomorrow evening, and yet it didn't look as if he was going to be back by then.

When he still wasn't in the office on Friday she didn't know what to do, and was tempted to ask James Courtney if he had any idea what had happened to Gideon, but was loath to invite his ridicule.

As it happened James Courtney brought the subject up himself as she was preparing to leave for the evening. 'Would you come into my office for a moment, Laura?' he requested.

'I—Yes, of course.' She looked awkwardly at Dorothy

and Janice as they both said hurried goodbyes. She had had to put up with a lot of conversations halting as she entered a room, a lot of knowing looks in her direction this last week, and James Courtney had just added to the speculation about her. Not that she thought Dorothy would make anything of it; she treated Laura with the same friendliness that she always had, her discretion seeming to include her now. But Janice was another story; she enjoyed the fact that she was actually working with the girl who was supposed to be dating Gideon Maitland.

'Stop looking annoyed,' James Courtney looked up to snap. 'God, you're a fiery little thing! I only want to pass on a message from Gideon. Although I'm not sure I should now. You——'

'From Gideon?' she interrupted eagerly. 'You've heard from Gideon?'

James Courtney frowned. 'Every day. Haven't you?'

'No,' she admitted reluctantly.

'Just as well,' he said tersely. 'Gideon's in Manchester to work, not to spend hours on the telephone talking to you.'

'Mr Courtney——'

'Miss Jamieson,' he mocked. 'Calm down, Laura, Gideon will be back tonight.'

Her expression brightened. 'He will?'

'Yes. Unfortunately not soon enough to escort you to the company dinner——'

'Oh.'

'You were going with him, I believe?'

'Yes,' she acknowledged, her disappointment acute. She had even been out and bought the new dress on the basis of Gideon's promise to take her. Well, he was coming back, but not in time for tonight's dinner.

'Now you're going with me,' James Courtney informed her with obvious pleasure.

Laura frowned. 'I am not!'

'And I thought you were a mousy little thing,' he

sighed, shaking his head. 'Do you love Gideon?' he asked suddenly.

Colour flooded her cheeks. 'I hardly know him,' she gasped. 'And I don't see what it has to do with you anyway.'

'I don't suppose you do. But Gideon has been like a son to me, I'd like to see him happy.'

Laura looked away. 'I don't think you should be discussing this with me.'

'Gideon gave me a different impression. *Do* you love him?'

'Yes!'

'Good,' he nodded his approval. 'You've met Lisa?' he added sharply, his gaze probing.

'Yes.'

Some of her dislike must have shown in her face, because James Courtney chuckled softly. 'You don't like her either, hmm?'

'I don't know her,' Laura replied tactfully.

James Courtney's mouth twisted with distaste. 'Five minutes of her company should be enough to tell you all you need to know about that young lady. Only Felicity and Gideon seem to have been blind to her faults, Felicity because she thought of her as a friend, Gideon—well, he has his own reasons, I would presume.'

'Probably.' Laura's voice was stilted.

James Courtney looked at her with narrowed blue eyes. 'She'll try to break you and Gideon up——'

'Mr Courtney——'

'Listen to me, Laura,' he said heatedly. 'I've known Lisa Harlow since almost before you were born, and there's nothing about her that I like. Unfortunately she has made herself indispensible to Gideon—where Natalie is concerned, and only where Natalie is concerned, I hope. I believe you've met my granddaughter.' His face softened.

Laura felt on safer ground now. 'Gideon and I took her

to the Zoo on Saturday.'

James Courtney chuckled. 'She loves that. Did you like her?' he asked suddenly.

'I lov—Mr Courtney, I would like to go home,' she said stiltedly. 'It's after five, and——'

'Get down off your high horse, young lady, and show some respect for your elders.' He quirked an eyebrow at her. 'Or don't you think I deserve respect?'

She bit her lip. 'It isn't that——'

'No,' he sighed. 'I'm being nosey, too damned nosey. Gideon wouldn't thank me for prying into his affairs. But I meant it about escorting you tonight.'

Laura shook her head. 'I'd rather not go.'

'Gideon will be joining us later,' he told her softly, watching for her reaction.

'He—he will?' she asked breathlessly, the world suddenly looking bright again.

James Courtney nodded. 'He could be half an hour late, possibly an hour, certainly no more than that. If I take you, he'll meet you there later.'

Now she didn't know what to do. Going to dinner with Gideon would have been bad enough, but actually arriving with James Courtney, the chairman of the company, would cause a sensation. But she desperately wanted to see Gideon . . .

'What time shall I call for you?' James Courtney made her decision for her.

'Seven-thirty.' She could hardly wait to see her mother's face!

After all she had told her mother about what a despot James Courtney was he had to be his most charming when she introduced the two of them later that evening!

'Gideon told me how beautiful you were,' he smiled, holding Laura's mother's hand longer than was necessary and smiling directly into her eyes. 'And he didn't exaggerate.'

'You're just being kind,' her mother blushed like a schoolgirl.

Laura shot James Courtney a look of impatience, but his blue eyes twinkled merrily as he returned that look. He was enjoying himself, the old devil!

'Shouldn't we be leaving?' she said pointedly. 'After all, you are the guest of honour.'

'Rubbish,' he dismissed. 'They would all be quite happy if I didn't turn up at all. They could all get drunk in comfort if I weren't here.'

'No doubt some of them will do that anyway,' she said dryly, remembering the way Martin had always come home inebriated from these affairs.

'No doubt,' he nodded agreement. 'You and I must meet again, Mrs Jamieson, when we have more time to talk.'

'Yes,' she agreed breathlessly, obviously as bowled over by James Courtney as Laura had been by Gideon.

'Mr Courtney,' Laura reminded him, never having seen her mother react so coyly to a man before.

'She's such a bossy young lady,' he told her mother, shaking his head.

Her mother looked scandalised. 'Surely not?'

He chuckled. 'Gideon tells me I bring out the worst in her, and from your reaction I think he must be right. But to tell you the truth,' he added conspiratorially, 'I like it,' he smiled.

In this mood he was irresistible, and Laura could see her mother was fascinated by him.

'You're a flirt,' she accused once she and James Courtney were in his limousine on their way to the dinner.

He chuckled with delight. 'There's life in the old man yet! And this old man thinks you look beautiful.'

She hoped Gideon thought so too. The dress she had bought was supposed to make her look older, attractively so. If Gideon liked sophistication then the green dress provided that—it was sleeveless, with very thin ribbon shoulder-straps, the neckline showing a creamy expanse of her breasts, fitting over their pertness to flare out in concertina pleats to just below her knees, the high heels on her sandals adding to her height. James Courtney's praise added to her confidence, and until Gideon arrived she would need all the moral support she could get. She wasn't exactly welcomed into her work colleagues' circle any more.

'You needn't flatter me,' she told James Courtney. 'I'm still not going to let you flirt with my mother,' she teased.

'She's a beautiful woman,' he smiled.

'I think so,' Laura nodded. 'But you're the last thing she needs in her life.'

He looked hurt. 'That isn't nice, Laura.'

'Neither are you most of the time.' Her look of sophistication gave her a cheeky humour—plus she was going to see Gideon! That was enough to make her feel ecstatic.

James Courtney was suddenly serious. 'I do like your mother, Laura. Would you really object if I were to see her again?'

Laura frowned her surprise. 'Do you want to?'

'As long as it isn't going to upset you,' he nodded. 'I wouldn't want to tread on any toes.'

Considering that he put people out of business without so much as a qualm she found his concern for her feelings very surprising. But then his ruthlessness in business didn't necessarily spill over into his private life, in fact his love for his granddaughter seemed to more than prove that.

She smiled at him. 'I have no objections as long as my mother doesn't,' she grinned. 'Why don't you ask her to go out with you and Natalie to the Zoo tomorrow? Oh, I'm sorry,' she blushed, 'that was a bit audacious of me.'

'As it happens I'm not taking Natalie to the Zoo, I'm taking her to see a friend of mine who owns a farm.'

'Oh, she'll like that!'

'But would your mother?' James asked dryly.

'She'll enjoy being with Natalie. She's a little disgusted with my brother and me for not marrying and providing her with grandchildren.'

'Then I'll telephone her in the morning.' He seemed pleased by the development, suddenly looking bashful. 'It must be forty years since I last asked a woman out on a date with me.'

'Then it's about time you did it again,' Laura teased. 'Anyway, *I'm* your date for this evening.'

He grimaced. 'Only until Gideon arrives, then I won't see you for dust.'

Laura blushed. Was she that obvious? She supposed she was. But she couldn't help it; Gideon was so much in her thoughts, especially tonight, when she hadn't seen him for almost a week. She was so keyed up about seeing him that she didn't even notice the speculative looks cast in her direction when she joined James at the top table, her whole attention was fixed on the doorway into this reception room in one of London's top hotels, just waiting for the moment Gideon arrived.

The meal passed miserably for her as she refused course after course of the delectable food. In the end the waiter seemed to be considering it a challenge to get her to eat something!

'For goodness' sake have some cheese,' James muttered. 'People are beginning to notice.'

She laughingly obliged, biting uninterestedly into a tangy Cheddar. 'Are you sure Gideon's going to be here tonight?' she asked. 'It's very late.'

'He'll be here,' James assured her softly.

'Yes, but when?' she sighed.

He shook his head, smiling. 'Patience isn't a virtue of youth.'

Gideon wasn't coming, she knew he wasn't coming. The dinner had all been cleared away, the band was now playing music they could all dance to, the drink started to

Say Hello to Yesterday
Holly Weston had done it all alone.

She had raised her small son and worked her way up to features writer for a major newspaper. Still the bitterness of the the past seven years lingered.

She had been very young when she married Nick Falconer—but old enough to lose her heart completely when he left. Despite her success in her new life, her old one haunted her.

But it was over and done with—until an assignment in Greece brought her face to face with Nick, and all she was trying to forget. . . .

Time of the Temptress
The game must be played his way!

Rebellion against a cushioned, controlled life had landed Eve Tarrant in Africa. Now only the tough mercenary Wade O'Mara stood between her and possible death in the wild, revolution-torn jungle.

But the real danger was Wade himself—he had made Eve aware of herself as a woman.

"I saved your neck, so you feel you owe me something," Wade said. "But you don't owe me a thing, Eve. Get away from me." She knew she could make him lose his head if she tried. But that wouldn't solve anything. . . .

Your Romantic Adventure Starts Here.

Born Out of Love
It had to be coincidence!

Charlotte stared at the man through a mist of confusion. It was Logan. An older Logan, of course, but unmistakably the man who had ravaged her emotions and then abandoned her all those years ago.

She ought to feel angry. She ought to feel resentful and cheated. Instead, she was apprehensive—terrified at the complications he could create.

"We are not through, Charlotte," he told her flatly. "I sometimes think we haven't even begun."

Man's World
Kate was finished with love for good.

Kate's new boss, features editor Eliot Holman, might have devastating charms—but Kate couldn't care less, even if it was obvious that he was interested in her.

Everyone, including Eliot, thought Kate was grieving over the loss of her husband, Toby. She kept it a carefully guarded secret just how cruelly Toby had treated her and how terrified she was of trusting men again.

But Eliot refused to leave her alone, which only served to infuriate her. He was no different from any other man. . . or was he?

These FOUR free Harlequin Presents novels allow you to enter the world of romance, love and desire. As a member of the Harlequin Home Subscription Plan, you can continue to experience all the moods of love. You'll be inspired by moments so real...so moving...you won't want them to end. So start your own Harlequin Presents adventure by returning the reply card below. <u>DO IT TODAY!</u>

TAKE THESE 4 BOOKS AND TOTE BAG FREE!

Mail to: Harlequin Reader Service
649 Ontario Street, Stratford, Ont. N5A 6W2

YES, please send me FREE and without obligation my 4 **Harlequin Presents** If you do not hear from me after I have examined my 4 FREE books, please send me the 8 new **Harlequin Presents** each month as soon as they come off the presses. I understand that I will be billed only $14.00 for all 8 books. There are no shipping and handling nor any other hidden charges. There is no minimum number of books that I have to purchase. In fact, I can cancel this arrangement at any time. The first 4 books and the tote bag are mine to keep as FREE gifts, even if I do not buy any additional books. CP195

MARIA DE FATIMA MEDEIROS
Name (please print)

53 WYDHAM St.
Address **Apt. No.**

TORONTO ONTARIO M6K K
City **Province** **Postal Code**

Don Juan
Signature (If under 18, parent or guardian must sign).

This offer is limited to one order per household and not valid to present subscribers. We reserve the right to exercise discretion in granting membership. If price changes are necessary you will be notified. Offer expires June 30, 1983.

PRINTED IN U.S.A.

Business Reply Mail
No Postage Stamp Necessary
if Mailed in Canada

Postage will be paid by

Harlequin Reader Service

649 Ontario Street

Stratford, Ontario

N5A 9Z9

Canada Post
Postes
Canada
021

flow freely, the lights were lowered.

'I hope Gideon arrives soon,' James growled, looking frowningly at his employees. 'I usually leave when it gets to this stage.'

He and Laura were sitting at a secluded table, James refusing all the invitations from the directors for them to join them. Laura hoped Gideon would arrive soon too, if he didn't she might as well leave with James Courtney.

'Excuse me, sir,' Nigel Jennings stood next to their table, 'may I borrow Laura for a dance?'

He received a piercing look for his trouble. 'Laura?' James growled.

'I'd love to.' She stood up in one fluid movement and followed Nigel on to the dance floor, the first real contact she had had with him since he had realised she was seeing Gideon.

'Maybe it isn't my place to say anything,' said Nigel after a few minutes of dancing together to the slow music, 'but aren't you getting in just a little too deep, Laura?' He looked down at her with concerned blue eyes.

She blushed, almost missing a step in her agitation. 'Sometimes it happens that way,' she dismissed lightly. 'It was a good meal, wasn't it?' she changed the subject.

'How would you know?' he sighed. 'You didn't eat anything.'

'You were watching me?' she gasped.

He nodded. 'And so was almost everyone else in the room. You and Gideon are the hottest piece of gossip to hit this company in a long time.'

'How nice!' she snapped her resentment.

'You would have been the same if it had been Janice he'd suddenly shown this interest in, now wouldn't you?'

She would have liked to have said no, but she knew the answer was really yes. The executives in a firm the size of Courtneys were always speculative subjects romantically. Hadn't she and Janice discussed Gideon's romantic interests before she actually became one of them?

'I suppose so,' she sighed her agreement.

'You know so,' he smiled. 'And talking of Gideon . . .' he was looking over her shoulder towards the doorway.

Her heart gave a sudden lurch, and she turned just in time to see Gideon joining James Courtney at their table. He looked so handsome, her heart just seemed to turn over, the burgundy-coloured velvet jacket tailored to the broadness of his shoulders, his shirt snowy white, the black trousers fitted to his muscular thighs.

Her gaze returned hungrily to his face, and she saw he was watching her in return, although he seemed to be carrying on a conversation with James, his eyes narrowed to grey slits, his expression cold. He certainly didn't look pleased to see her.

Nigel sighed. 'You want me to take you back to the table, right?'

Laura glanced at Gideon once more, his face remote as he relaxed back in his chair. He looked like a stranger, a cold, hard stranger. 'We'll finish the dance,' she said firmly.

'Sure?' he frowned down at her.

'Very sure,' she nodded. 'And don't frown like that—people will think you aren't enjoying dancing with me.'

'By "people" I take it you mean Gideon,' he said dryly.

'I mean people,' she said stubbornly.

'All right,' Nigel laughed softly. 'But I hope you know what you're doing. Gideon hasn't seemed too keen on your being with me in the past.'

Considering he had been away for the past week and hadn't attempted to even telephone her once she considered one dance was the least she owed herself. She couldn't appear too eager, no matter how she longed to run back to the table.

'This tune is one of my favourites,' she invented, never

having remembered hearing it before.

'I'll bet,' Nigel drawled, not fooled for one minute.

It took all her willpower to continue dancing until the music came to an end; she was conscious of Gideon watching her the whole time, his expression unreadable.

'That was lovely, thank you.' She gave Nigel a glowing smile, stepping back to take her leave.

He returned the smile. 'If I believed that you preferred dancing with me to being with Gideon I'd be a happy man. But I've never been one to deceive myself.'

'Nigel——'

'Come on,' he put his arm about her waist, leading her off the dance floor, 'at least let me have the pleasure of seeing Gideon jealous.'

'Nigel——' she began again.

He grinned down at her. 'Don't take it all so seriously, Laura. It won't hurt him to have a little competition.'

She was beginning to get the impression that Nigel had had a little too much to drink, he would certainly never have contemplated challenging Gideon in this way normally.

James Courtney and Gideon both stood up as she and Nigel approached the table, and Laura's gaze instantly fixed on Gideon's brooding features. He didn't look very welcoming!

'One beautiful lady safely returned,' Nigel said lightly, his arm still about her waist. 'Glad you could join us, Gideon.'

'So am I,' Gideon drawled, sitting down again now.

'If you hadn't,' Nigel continued, 'I just might have stolen Laura for myself.'

Laura held her breath at Nigel's deliberate baiting of the other man. He didn't look drunk, but then you didn't have to be near collapsing point to have had too much to drink.

'Indeed?' Gideon wasn't going to be baited, that much

was obvious by his cool attitude.

Nigel realised that much at least, making his excuses. 'Maybe we could have another dance together later, Laura.' He couldn't seem to resist this parting shot.

'Maybe,' she agreed, finally able to sit down now that he had removed his arm, watching as he walked back across the room to join his friends.

James Courtney stood up. 'I hope you'll excuse me. I just want to have a word with Bill Davies, and then I'm on my way.'

'You aren't leaving?' Laura felt strangely shy about being left alone with Gideon, especially when he was in this unapproachable mood.

'I am,' he grimaced. 'Would you tell your mother I'll be calling her in the morning?'

'Of course,' she smiled, but the smile died once he had left, and she looked anywhere but at Gideon now that they had been left alone together. The last time they had been together she had told him she loved him, and now she was unsure how to act with him.

'What was that remark about your mother?' he enquired casually, lighting up a cheroot.

Laura's smile was completely natural as she thought of James' attraction to her mother. 'Your father-in-law wants to invite my mother out for the day tomorrow,' she explained.

Gideon seemed to stiffen. 'The two of them have met, then?' he said tautly.

She nodded. 'Tonight.'

He seemed to relax with effort, the smoke from his cheroot surrounding him like a cloak. 'I had a feeling James would like your mother. How was your week?' he changed the subject.

'Busy,' she shrugged. 'Although we're just about back to full force now.'

He nodded. 'So James told me.'

She had known things were going to be a bit strained between them after a week of not seeing each other, but she hadn't expected them to be like two strangers making polite conversation! 'How was your week?'

'Also busy.' He knocked ash off his cheroot, looking lazily attractive as he surveyed the other people in the room. He suddenly turned cold grey eyes on her. 'Did yours happen to be "busy" with Nigel Jennings?' he rasped.

Laura jumped nervously with the abruptness of the question. 'Nigel?' she blinked.

'Yes,' he bit out. 'Have you been seeing him this week?'

'No, of course not. But I seem to remember you told me it was none of your business what I did when I wasn't with you.' Her eyes flashed her rebellion.

'And I seem to remember that was before you told me you loved me.'

Colour flooded her cheeks. 'That wasn't fair!' she choked.

'No one ever said love was that,' he mocked.

Laura swallowed hard, her hands twisting together. 'It wasn't very fair of you to make me admit my feelings for you either,' especially when he hadn't reciprocated!

'It wasn't?'

'No, it wasn't!' she flashed. 'And if you have nothing better to do than be tormenting, I have!' She stood up. 'I'm sure Nigel would be very pleased if I were to join him.'

'I'm sure he would,' Gideon also stood up, 'but I happen to have other plans for you.' His grasp on her arm held her to his side. 'And they include me,' he added softly.

She gulped. 'They—they do?'

'Yes. Let's get out of here,' he muttered. 'A week is a hell of a long time.'

Laura blushed with the undue haste with which Gideon hurried her from the hotel and out to the car that had been brought round for them.

'Gideon . . .' She turned to look at him dazedly.

'Yes?' he asked tautly, as the Jaguar cut through the traffic.

'I—What's the matter?'

He gave her a sideways glance. 'I'll tell you in a moment.'

'In a moment' was when they had parked outside Laura's home, and he didn't tell her, he showed her, switching off the engine to turn and pull her into his arms, his kiss savage in its intensity. All the breath seemed to be knocked out of her body as he forced her back against the door, his lips devouring her hungrily.

'Gideon!' she gasped weakly when he at last released her lips to place heated kisses down her throat and creamy shoulders.

He drew back with a ragged sigh, resting his forehead on hers. 'I needed that,' he breathed deeply. 'I never realised a week could be so long.'

'You didn't?'

'No,' he smiled, gently touching her parted lips, a slight swelling there already beginning to show the fierceness of his kiss. 'I'm sorry,' he said huskily. 'It seems I can never be gentle with you. But I'm usually wanting you so badly gentleness doesn't enter into it. I didn't mean to hurt you just now, but when I arrived tonight and saw you with Jennings . . .!' He shook his head. 'It didn't exactly induce calm to my already tense mood,' he told her ruefully.

Laura touched the hardness of his cheek, gazing up at him adoringly. So that haughty coldness had hidden a burning anger. Would she ever know this man completely? 'Why were you feeling tense?' she teased, already guessing the reason; his passion of a few minutes ago had been unmistakable.

His eyes glowed in the darkness. 'Is your mother waiting up for you?'

Laura shook her head. 'She isn't even at home.' She glanced at the watch on her wrist. 'She won't be home for another hour at least.'

Something like a groan escaped his throat. 'Ask me up to your flat for coffee and I'll show you why I was so tense.'

'For coffee . . .?' She gave him a mocking look, so glad to have the Gideon she loved back in evidence.

'Forget the coffee,' he groaned huskily. 'Just ask me into your home.'

She gave him a considering look, her fingers running teasingly down the rigid line of his jaw. 'I'm not sure I should . . .'

'Ask me in, damn you,' he advised in a growl. 'Unless you want to make love in the back seat of a car!'

She smiled at his fierceness, uncaring that he actually meant what he said. 'All right, you're duly invited.'

He sat back with a sigh. 'Thank God for that!'

Laura was very conscious of his possessive hold on her waist as they went up to her flat, and her fingers fumbled in her handbag for her doorkey as she anticipated the next hour in his arms.

The door swung open before she could manage to fit the key properly into the lock. 'Martin!' she gasped, for amazingly her brother stood there, so dear it brought tears to her eyes, her pleasure in seeing him making her forget the reason Gideon was with her.

She sensed rather than felt the tension between the two men as they looked at each other, the hostility between them unmistakable, the air seeming to crackle with their mutual dislike.

CHAPTER SIX

LAURA moved to give her brother a hug, stepping back with a puzzled frown when she saw that he and Gideon were still looking at each other warily. It wasn't like Martin not to like anyone, he didn't usually have time for such things, being too busy enjoying life to bother with such an emotion. But he certainly wasn't pleased to see Gideon, and the feeling seemed to be mutual, the ardent lover of a few minutes ago completely erased by harshness.

'Martin, this is——'

'I know who he is,' he rasped in a voice completely unlike his usual friendly tone. 'What are you doing with my sister, Maitland?' He pulled Laura to his side, glaring at the other man with dark brown eyes, his dark good looks rakishly attractive, making him very popular with the opposite sex.

'Martin!' she gasped, pulling out of his grasp. 'Martin, you can't talk to Gideon like that,' she looked at him pleadingly.

'Can't I?' he said grimly. 'Oh, I think I can. I asked you a question, Maitland.'

'One that doesn't require an answer,' Gideon drawled a reply, completely at ease and in control. 'It must be obvious that I've just brought Laura home after an evening out together.'

Martin's mouth twisted angrily. 'And why are you taking my sister out at all?'

'Surely that's obvious too?' he mocked.

'It is to me,' Martin's eyes glittered furiously. 'But I doubt it is to Laura.'

Cool grey eyes were turned on her as she looked on in bewilderment. It was strange enough that Martin should come home unexpectedly like this without telling anyone of his plans, but his behaviour towards Gideon, and Gideon's reaction to it, was even more puzzling.

'I'm sure Laura knows exactly why I'm taking her out,' Gideon drawled.

'I doubt it,' Martin snapped.

'But you do?' he returned coolly.

'Yes, I do! And I won't let you do it, Maitland. I won't let you hurt Laura the way you hurt——'

'That's the past, Jamieson,' Gideon cut in coldly, an angry sheen to his slate-grey eyes. 'And I wasn't the one who did the hurting.'

Laura still didn't know what was going on, and she thought it was about time that she did. 'Martin——'

'Stay out of this, Laura,' her brother didn't even look at her. 'This has nothing to do with you.'

'On the contrary,' Gideon corrected harshly, 'I think it has everything to do with Laura.'

'Only because you made it so,' Martin accused.

'No,' Gideon shook his head. '*You're* making it so. Laura has no need to know about the past.'

'She does when it's the only reason you've been taking her out. Well, I won't let you hurt my sister,' Martin snarled. 'When I went to America I made it clear that you would hear no more from me. You're the one who's dragged the past out into the open. And this time I'm not going to take it, not when you've involved Laura.'

'Martin, please——'

'I think he's right, Laura,' Gideon told her softly. 'For the moment it would be better if you stayed out of this. Your brother seems to have an inflated opinion of his importance——'

'Not inflated, Maitland. I don't consider fifty thousand pounds inflated at all,' Martin scorned.

Gideon seemed to go grey. 'What the hell are you talking about?'

Martin's mouth twisted bitterly. 'My pay-off. Well, now I'm giving you the pay-off—stay away from my sister, or I'll make sure it all comes out.'

Gideon took a threatening step towards him, checking himself at the last. 'I have no idea what you're talking about——'

Martin's scornful laugh interrupted him. 'You know all right. Well, I may not care for much in this life, and I may be a bastard, but you're an even bigger one. Laura is completely innocent of all this, and I'm not going to let you hurt her.'

'I haven't——'

'Not yet,' Martin said grimly. 'But you would have done. And we both know why, don't we?'

'Do we?' Gideon sighed.

'Oh yes,' Martin nodded. 'And maybe she should know too. That way I won't have to make her stay away from you, she won't want to come anywhere near you.'

'Why drag all this up?' Gideon rasped. 'Laura hasn't been hurt——'

'And she isn't going to be!'

'Martin!' Laura at last cried her bewilderment, her face very pale. 'Would you please tell me what's going on?'

'Revenge is what's going on,' he revealed tightly.

'Revenge?' she frowned. 'For what?'

'For the fact that I had an affair with his wife.'

'Wh-what did you say?' she gasped faintly, dropping down into the nearest armchair, gazing dazedly up at Gideon's harshness and Martin's fury.

'Felicity Maitland and I had an affair,' her brother told her tautly. 'Now *he* intends having an affair with you.'

Gideon's mouth twisted. 'Why should you think you

would be any more worthy of revenge than all the others?'

'Others?' For a moment Martin looked taken aback. 'There were no others!'

'I could prove to you that there were——'

'No doubt you could,' Martin's mouth twisted. 'No doubt men like you could "prove" a lot of things if you chose to.'

'Jamieson——'

'Gideon,' Laura at last found her voice, hardly able to believe what she was hearing. 'Gideon, is this true?' She had a feeling she knew the answer before he told it to her; it would explain so many things, his interest in a little nobody like her for a start.

'Parts of it are,' he sighed. 'But not the bit about you and me——'

'You and me?' her voice cracked shrilly. 'There is no you and me!'

'Laura——'

'You heard her,' Martin snarled. 'It didn't work out, Maitland, just accept that.'

'I'll accept nothing!' Gideon exploded into anger, the temper Laura's mother had only guessed at much in evidence. 'Laura and I have nothing to do with the fact that you and my wife had an affair. You can think what you like about Felicity, I couldn't give a damn any more. But I won't have you twisting the facts to Laura. Laura——'

'Stay away from me!' She cringed away from the hand he put out to her.

'Laura——'

'Stay away from her, Maitland!' Martin pushed him away.

Gideon spun round, his eyes glittering with rage. 'Don't ever do that again,' he said coldly. 'Not if you want to keep your face looking that way.'

His coldness had more effect than the physical violence he threatened, and Martin backed a safe distance away.

Gideon came down on his haunches in front of Laura, not touching her, but looking as if he would like to. 'Laura, you have to believe me,' he said gently.

'I can't!' she shook her head, the tears that she had been holding back cascading freely down her cheeks. 'It explains so much—the sudden way you asked me out, the way you deliberately set out to make me attracted to you, the—the way you made me admit my love for you,' she finished in a hushed voice.

He sighed. 'There's a much more simple explanation if only you would care to see it. Come with me, Laura. Let me explain——'

'I think you've explained enough for one evening,' Martin dismissed angrily. 'And from what I've heard I only just got home in time. Laura won't be working for you any more——'

'Oh yes, I will,' she interrupted firmly, surprising both men. She wiped the tears away with the back of her hand. 'If and when I leave Courtneys it won't be because I was forced to.' She stood up. 'Now if you'll both excuse me, your argument no longer concerns me.'

'Laura, for God's sake!'

She didn't even turn at the pleading in Gideon's voice, maintaining her dignity until she was safely in her room. Then all the fight went out of her, leaving her weak and defenceless.

Martin and Felicity Maitland! She could hardly believe it, and yet she knew it was true. And Gideon had been using her to get his revenge for that affair. All the time she had felt there was something wrong with their relationship, had sensed Gideon's reserve, and yet she would never have guessed his often cold manner could hide such cruelty.

He had set out to make her fall in love with him, his

pursuit had been ruthless in its intent, and tonight would probably have been his ultimate revenge. Laura had no doubt that if Martin hadn't been here to tell her the things he had that she and Gideon would even now have been making love together.

She could still hear raised voices in the other room, the two men were obviously still arguing. Then the front door slammed, and she knew Gideon had left.

A knock sounded on her bedroom door before Martin walked in. 'Can I talk to you?' he asked gently.

She looked up at him from her lying position on the bed, her misery obvious. 'Is there anything left to say?' she choked.

'I think so.' He sat down beside her.

'Why did you come back, Martin?' her voice broke. 'Why did you have to spoil it all?'

'I didn't spoil it, love,' he shook his head. 'There wasn't really anything to spoil. Maitland was using you. You didn't want that, did you?'

She bit her bottom lip to stop it trembling. 'How did you know—about Gideon and me?'

'Mum wrote and told me, she seemed quite pleased about it. When you wrote and told me you were going to work at Courtneys I felt a bit apprehensive, but when Mum told me you were actually going out with Gideon Maitland . . .! I got the first plane home.'

Laura swallowed down the tears, drying her cheeks with a tissue as she sat up beside her brother. 'Tell me—tell me about you and—and Felicity.'

He sighed. 'There isn't much to tell, Maitland saw to that.'

'But how did you ever meet her?'

'At a company dinner three years ago.'

Laura choked with the irony of that. Who knew what would have happened after this company dinner if Martin hadn't been here?

'She was very unhappy with Maitland,' Martin continued.

'Why?'

He shook his head. 'Felicity didn't even like to talk about him.'

'You and she were—very close?'

'Very,' he confirmed, a ruddy hue colouring his cheeks. 'For about three months, until Maitland found out and put a stop to it. I was in love with Felicity, I wanted to marry her.'

'Did—did you know she died?'

He stood up forcefully, his hands clenched at his sides. 'Yes, I—I heard about that. Lisa and I kept in touch.'

'Lisa . . .?' she echoed weakly.

'Lisa Harlow. She was the only friend Felicity and I had.'

Laura couldn't believe Lisa Harlow had ever been a friend to anyone but herself. 'How?' she asked huskily.

'She was our go-between. Felicity and I used to arrange to see each other through her.'

Laura frowned. It seemed to her that no matter what happened Lisa Harlow was in the centre of it, seeming almost to control the people around her. The other woman had encouraged Felicity's affair with Martin, and yet Gideon trusted her implicitly, had put the care of his child into her hands.

'But somehow Maitland found out,' Martin scowled.

Could Lisa have had anything to do with that too? It was possible she had, after all, she wanted Gideon for herself, and if Felicity left Gideon for another man the field would be clear for her. Only it hadn't worked out that way. Felicity had stayed with Gideon, had given him a daughter.

'What happened?' she asked softly.

Martin's expression became savage. 'Maitland tried to buy me off——'

'The fifty thousand pounds!' she gasped.

'Yes, damn him! Of course I didn't take it, instead I left. Felicity was so sweet and—and innocent. I know how that sounds, she and Maitland had been married for years, but there was something so—so untouched about her. She'd been protected and spoilt all her life, first by her father and then by Maitland, while I had nothing to offer her. Oh, it was all made clear to me,' he said bitterly. 'So I left, went to America. And then Lisa wrote and told me Felicity was dead,' his voice broke emotionally. 'I should have taken her with me, but I had nothing to offer her, none of the luxury she'd been used to all her life. All I had was a life of poverty. I couldn't do that to her.'

'Oh, Martin!' She went to him, putting her arms about him. 'I'm so sorry. We—Mum and I, never realised what you went through. You always seemed such a flirt.'

'I was—I am. But I did love Felicity.'

And now she loved Gideon—and he had only been intent on hurting her. When would he have told her the truth?' Tonight, after he had made love to her?

'Maitland is a bastard,' Martin said savagely, as if reading her thoughts. 'All he cares about, all he's ever cared about, is having possession of Courtneys. He couldn't let Felicity leave him, not if he wanted to take over from James Courtney when the time came, so he got her pregnant.'

Laura gasped at the hatred in her brother's voice. Could this last bit possibly be true, or was it the angry dislike of a man who had lost the woman he loved? It could be a little of both. After all, Felicity and Gideon were husband and wife, and accidental pregnancies were known to happen even in this day and age of easily available contraceptives. All that Felicity's pregnancy proved was that their reconciliation had been successful.

'Mum isn't to know about all this,' Martin warned her. 'It would only upset her.'

She could see that. 'But what do we tell her about your sudden appearance?' she frowned.

He shrugged. 'Maybe—I know! Tell her we conspired to give her a surprise for her birthday next week. She'll believe that.'

Not surprisingly, she did, and the subject of Felicity and Gideon Maitland was forgotten once their mother arrived home. Mrs Jamieson was ecstatic about having her son home, if only for a brief holiday.

It wasn't until she had been in bed several minutes that Laura remembered James Courtney's message to her mother. Her mother was still preparing for bed when Laura entered her room.

'Isn't it lovely having Martin home,' she smiled happily.

'Yes,' she agreed with more meaning than her mother could possibly understand. If he hadn't come home when he had . . . But he had, and she wouldn't think about what might have happened.

Her mother seemed to notice her preoccupation for the first time. 'Anything wrong, dear?' she frowned.

'No, nothing,' she gave a bright smile. 'Mr Courtney was very taken with you.'

Her mother blushed prettily. 'He's a very distinguished man, isn't he?'

'At the moment he's a very smitten distinguished man,' Laura teased. 'So much so that he wants to take you out tomorrow.'

'He does?' her mother gasped.

'Mm. He's going to telephone you in the morning. He wondered if you would like to spend the day with him and Natalie.'

'She's such a beautiful child. Did Gideon manage to make it this evening?'

Laura looked away. 'Yes, he was there. But he was very late getting back from Manchester.'

Her mother looked concerned, seeming to sense her mood of reserve. 'You and he haven't argued, have you?'

'Well, I—Yes,' Laura admitted reluctantly. 'Um—Gideon took exception to the time I spent with Nigel Jennings,' she invented.

'Oh, he'll get over that,' her mother dismissed. 'If he's jealous then he must be serious,' she added thoughtfully.

'No——'

'Oh yes, Laura,' she smiled. 'Not that a little jealousy will hurt him. He's altogether too sure of himself.'

'You don't understand, Mum. Gideon and I—we aren't—Well——'

'He'll come round,' her mother assured her. 'You'll see, he'll be on the telephone first thing tomorrow morning.'

'No, he won't,' Laura shook her head. 'And I don't want him to be.'

'Of course you do——'

'No, I don't. You see, I've found I prefer Nigel Jennings——'

'*Who* is Nigel Jennings?' her mother interrupted impatiently. 'Where on earth did you meet him?'

'He works at Courtneys too.'

'And you prefer him to Gideon?' Her mother made it sound as if that couldn't be possible.

'He's much less complex, and——'

'And boring, I should think. You can't mean it, Laura,' her mother sounded scandalised.

'I do,' she said firmly.

'But, Laura——'

'I'm sorry, Mum, but that's the way I feel. But that doesn't stop you going out with Mr Courtney.' She hoped Nigel would forgive her for using his name in this way, but she knew she would be more believable if her mother thought she was interested in someone else.

'It most certainly doesn't. Well, I liked him too,' she blushed at Laura's teasing look.

'And why shouldn't you, he's a very attractive man.' Laura moved to the door.

'Laura . . .'

'Mm?' she turned.

'About Gideon——'

'I told you, I won't be seeing him again.'

'But, Laura——'

'Please, Mum,' she sighed, her nerves stretched to breaking point, 'I'm tired, I want to go to bed.'

'But I don't understand——'

'There's nothing to understand. It's over between Gideon and me,' her voice broke emotionally.

'You don't sound as if you want it to be.'

'Well, I do.' And if she didn't soon get to the privacy of her bedroom she was going to prove just what a liar she was by bursting into tears!

Her mother shrugged. 'Did Mr Courtney say what time he would telephone?'

'About ten,' and Laura hurriedly made her escape.

She still couldn't believe it had happened. Gideon should have been an actor, his performance this evening as the jealous lover had been most convincing, so much so that she would probably have been prepared to let him make love to her to show him how unnecessary his jealousy was.

She had no idea how she was going to face him again, all she knew was that she was going to do it! And she would do it proudly. Perhaps Nigel wouldn't mind helping her.

James Courtney telephoned promptly at ten o'clock the next morning, and their mother had long gone by the time Martin emerged yawning from his bedroom.

'The flight,' he excused his lateness. 'No Mum?'

Laura avoided his eyes, drinking her coffee. 'She's gone out with a friend for the day.' She was reluctant to tell him who with, having no reason to suppose he liked James Courtney any more than he did Gideon.

Martin sat down opposite her at the kitchen table. 'You look like I feel.'

'I also feel like I look,' she grimaced.

'I'm sorry, love,' he sighed. 'It's all my fault.'

She shook her head. 'It's no one's fault but my own. I should have known Gideon wouldn't be seriously interested in me.'

'You didn't really mean it about staying on at Courtneys, did you?'

'I did,' she told him firmly.

'But you can't——'

'I can, and I will.'

'Laura, I admire your spirit. But Maitland can make your life hell if he wants to.'

'I don't work for Gideon, I work for James Courtney.'

Martin scowled. 'Who believes his son-in-law can do no wrong. He worshipped Felicity, but even he couldn't see any wrong in Gideon Maitland, not even when he must have known how unhappy Felicity was with him.'

It seemed to Laura that if Felicity Maitland had been that unhappy she would have left Gideon no matter what. But it wasn't for her to point out such a thing to Martin, not when he was obviously still hurting so badly. But she had been right about his dislike of James Courtney too; thank God she hadn't told him their mother was out with him at this very moment!

Martin drained the coffee in his cup. 'I have some people to see today. You'll be all right on your own?'

'Fine,' she nodded, wondering if Lisa Harlow was one of the 'people' he had to see. 'How long will you be staying in England?'

He shrugged. 'I'm not sure. Long enough to see Maitland stays way from you.'

She gave a rueful smile. 'I'm a big girl now, Martin.

I'm not going to make that mistake again.'

'Maitland can be very persuasive,' he said bitterly. 'Why do you think Felicity stayed with him for so long?'

She sighed, no longer interested in why Felicity Maitland had done the things she had. 'Martin, I'm no longer four years old and you fifteen. I'm grown up now, I have to make my own mistakes and learn by them.' Ever since she could remember Martin had been around to pick up the pieces when she had faltered and fallen. And it was time it stopped, time she stood on her own two feet, even if she fell flat on her face.

Martin obviously didn't have the time to argue with her; he went to his room to change before going out.

When the telephone rang Laura had a premonition it was Gideon. She didn't answer it. Why couldn't he leave her alone, admit that he had lost!

An hour later the doorbell rang—and rang—and rang. It was Gideon, she knew it was him, had checked to see if his car was parked outside. It was.

'Laura, open this door!' he ordered firmly. 'I know you're in there,' he added softly.

He couldn't know any such thing unless she actually answered him—and she had no intention of doing that.

'Laura, for God's sake!' his voice was hoarse. 'Your brother and Felicity have nothing to do with us.'

Goodness, if he didn't stop shouting the neighbours would be coming out to investigate. 'Go away!' she hissed.

She heard him sigh his relief. 'Let me in, Laura,' he persuaded. 'We can talk.'

'We have nothing to say to each other. Now if you wouldn't mind leaving, I have a date this afternoon,' she invented.

'With Nigel Jennings?' he rasped.

'Who else?' she taunted.

She could hear no sound from the other side of the

closed door, holding her breath as she waited for Gideon's reaction. She finally heard him move away, the opening of the lift doors, the sound of its descent telling her that he had gone. As she ran over to the window she saw him get into his car, his expression grim.

Well, he had gone, and this time for good. Then why didn't she feel happier?

She had tea ready when her mother returned with James Courtney, laying the sleepy Natalie down in the bedroom before joining the other couple in the lounge.

'Did you have a good day?' she smiled.

'Very good,' James answered her. 'Do you have any sugar?' He looked down at the tea-tray.

'I'll get you some.' Laura rose to get it. The omission of sugar had been a deliberate one, as she and her mother did not take sweetening. And neither did James!

'I'll go,' her mother offered, and disappeared into the kitchen before Laura could stop her.

'My mother seems to have enjoyed herself,' Laura instantly launched into speech. 'She has so much colour in her cheeks——'

'Laura——'

'And Natalie obviously had a lovely time.' The little dungaree-clad figure had been covered in dirt, but glowing with health, her cheeks rosy. 'Did you——'

'Laura, shut up,' James growled. 'The merits of the day can be discussed in a moment. Your mother tells me that you and Gideon have had a—disagreement.'

Her mother had told him! No wonder she was taking so long to get the unwanted sugar. 'Whether we have or not——'

'Don't tell me it's none of my business,' James scowled, 'because I'm making it so. Now, what's he done to upset you?'

Remembering how everyone had said James Courtney idolised his daughter she knew the truth could never be told to this man. And his affection for Gideon was a genuine one, the two men seemed almost like father and son. James Courtney had lost his daughter, he didn't deserve to lose her memory too.

'Gideon is too arrogant——'

'Of course he's arrogant,' James interrupted impatiently. 'I wouldn't think him a worthy successor if he weren't. What else is wrong with him—in your opinion?' He made it sound as if that weren't worth much.

'He's autocratic——'

James raised his eyes heavenwards. 'I was expecting an attempted rape at least when your mother told me you were annoyed with him.'

'Sorry to disappoint you!' she flashed. 'But I would say Gideon is too cold to ever attempt to rape anyone.'

'So that's it,' he sighed. 'He hasn't been passionate enough for you. Have you ever thought he might respect you too much to try something like that?'

It was so far from the truth that she could have cried. 'Mr Courtney——'

'Call me James, girl,' he ordered. 'Some of the things you've said to me in the past make the formality ludicrous.'

She flushed. 'I'm sorry——'

'And don't apologise,' he snapped. 'I can't abide a woman who keeps apologising for her existence.'

'I'm not apologising for my existence!' she shouted. 'I'm just——'

'Laura!' her mother came hurriedly into the room. 'I won't have you talking to James in that way!'

'I don't mind, Joan,' he grinned. 'Most of the young women talk that way nowadays. Now, Laura——'

'The subject of Gideon is closed!' Laura stood up angrily. 'Very much so as far as I'm concerned.'

'But——'

'If you want to know any more, Mr Courtney, I suggest

you discuss it with Gideon. Excuse me,' and she went into her bedroom, quite forgetting that Natalie was lying on her bed asleep. The little girl looked so angelic, her long lashes fanned out across her chubby cheeks, her arms stretched in abandon as she slept in complete ignorance of the chaos her father had caused in Laura's life.

CHAPTER SEVEN

WHEN Natalie woke up she took her through to the lounge, helping the little girl to a drink of milk. Gideon had no right to have such a lovely daughter, he certainly didn't deserve her.

'She likes you.'

Laura looked up into James Courtney's eyes. For once the elderly man's mood softened. 'Natalie likes everyone,' she retorted stiltedly, standing up to hand the little girl to her grandfather. 'Even her father,' she added bitterly.

'Laura——'

'Excuse me,' she said coldly. 'I have some things to do in my bedroom.'

'Young lady, you are going to listen——'

'I think Natalie might be hungry,' she told her mother, ignoring James Courtney.

'Cake,' the little girl obliged her by saying.

'She understands food all right,' her grandfather said proudly.

Laura went back to her bedroom, leaving the older couple to feed the little girl. She just wanted today to be over, wished it were two or three months hence when the pain perhaps wouldn't be so bad. At least, she hoped it wouldn't! Did anyone ever get over loving someone as much as she loved Gideon?

She heard James Courtney take his leave about half an hour later, and half expected her mother's knock when it came a few minutes later. But she didn't get the reprimand she had been expecting.

'Gideon has really hurt you, hasn't he?' her mother said gently.

Tears filled Laura's eyes at her mother's understanding. 'Yes,' she admitted huskily.

'I thought so,' her mother nodded. 'You aren't acting like my Laura at all.'

She gave a watery smile. 'I'll apologise to Mr Courtney on Monday.'

'He's worried about you too.'

'Yes.' And she knew he was. Underneath all the bluff manner James Courtney was a bit of a softie. He didn't have a heart of gold or anything like that, that would be asking too much, but he was certainly more human than he let most people realise. 'Did you have a nice day?' she asked, to change the subject.

'Very nice,' her mother blushed.

'And are you seeing him again?'

'I—I thought I might. Do you think I should?'

'Do you still like him?'

'Yes.'

'Then of course you should see him,' Laura smiled.

'I hoped you'd say that. Do you think Martin would mind?'

'I—er—I shouldn't tell Martin just yet.' With the anger he had towards James Courtney he definitely wouldn't approve! 'After all,' she added lightly, 'he doesn't ask you if you mind who he dates.' He certainly hadn't told them about Felicity Maitland.

'I suppose not,' her mother agreed slowly. 'I could just be making more of it than there is.'

Much as she wanted her mother to be happy, to possibly marry again, Laura selfishly hoped it wouldn't be to James Courtney. If anything permanent were to come of that relationship she would have to see Gideon more than she wanted to, because James Courtney regarded him as a son.

Could James Courtney have known of his daughter's affair with Martin? It didn't seem very likely; he wouldn't have anything to do with them now if he had known.

They hardly saw Martin all weekend to tell him anything, he was out visiting friends most of the time, most of them female, as far as Laura could make out. He certainly didn't seem heartbroken for Felicity Maitland. Still, who was she to judge? Most men were adept at hiding their true feelings, a lesson she had learnt the hard way.

She went out herself on Sunday, just in case Gideon should come round or telephone. She wasn't sure if she was disappointed or relieved when her mother told her there had been no word from him. She told herself she was relieved, and yet the ache in her heart denied that.

Going to work on Monday morning was possibly the hardest thing she had ever done in her life. And yet she had to do it, had to show Gideon that he meant nothing to her—even if it weren't true. Besides, she wasn't a coward, and she wouldn't run away from this situation.

James Courtney gave her a searching look as he passed through the office, although he didn't say anything. If he had tried to speak to Gideon about their break-up he had probably been told for a second time to mind his own business.

'Did you have a good time on Friday?' Janice asked her.

'Very nice,' she replied without enthusiasm.

'Mr Maitland looked gorgeous. You lucky thing!' Janice eyed her almost questioningly.

'He did look handsome,' Laura agreed, then concentrated on her work.

'It was a shame he arrived so late.'

'Yes.'

'I suppose he was still in Manchester,' Janice probed, obviously storing up all Laura's answers ready to pass on to the rest of the staff.

Laura looked up with a sigh. 'Look, you might as well know that——'

'Laura, could you come out here, please,' requested an authoritative voice.

Her face paled, her eyes suddenly deeply green as she looked up at Gideon. He looked very pale and gaunt himself, not at all the assured man she was used to. But if he felt guilty about his treatment of her she felt no sympathy for him, but could only look at him with cold eyes.

'Laura,' he repeated abruptly, opening the door wider to the corridor.

She got up, not willing to show any sign of antagonism to him in front of Janice and Dorothy, and followed him outside before she spoke. 'What do you want?' she asked coldly.

'You know damn well what I want,' he groaned, his hands coming out to grasp her upper arms.

'Take your hands off me,' she ordered emotionlessly.

'Laura, for God's sake——'

'Let go of me!'

His hands dropped to his sides. 'Let me explain——'

'All the explaining that was necessary was done on Friday night—by my brother. Martin told me everything.'

Gideon's face darkened. 'Then I wish he would tell it to me. That fifty thousand pounds, for example—I have no idea what he's talking about.'

Laura's mouth twisted. 'You know,' she scorned. 'You just aren't willing to admit it.'

His face tightened with anger. 'I don't lie, Laura——'

'Oh, you lie!' She gave a bitter laugh, self-derisory. 'You let me, you let everyone, believe that you loved your wife.'

'No!' he shook his head. 'I never, ever, told you that.'

'You didn't need to. The way you act, your remoteness—it all gives the impression of a man with a broken heart. But you didn't love Felicity, if you had she would never have turned to Martin.' No woman in her right mind would prefer another man if she had Gideon for a husband, a loving husband. It might be disloyal to her brother to think this way, but although he was good-looking in a rakish sort of way he was no competition for

Gideon, not in a normal, happily married situation.

'You're right,' Gideon sighed heavily, 'I didn't love Felicity.'

Martin's accusation that Gideon had stayed with Felicity so that he could one day take control of Courtneys no longer seemed so improbable, and Laura recoiled from him. 'Just as you didn't love me.' Her mouth twisted. 'You love a woman when it suits your purpose to do so, for reasons I can't even begin to comprehend.'

'No!' his denial came out as a groan.

'You disgust me,' she told him coldly, suddenly feeling numb. Somewhere in the depths of her heart she had been hoping that he would deny it all, that he had another reason for taking her out. But that was all over now, her last hope was gone. 'Now if you'll excuse me, I have to get back to work . . .'

'We have to talk, Laura,' once again he grasped her arms, 'but not here. Come out with me tonight, and——'

'I wouldn't go anywhere with you, tonight or any other time,' she told him curtly.

'You love me!' he said fiercely, his fingers digging into her flesh, his eyes glittering deeply grey. 'Laura, you *love* me!'

'Do I?'

He seemed to pale at the lack of emotion in her voice, his hands falling away, his frown almost one of hurt puzzlement. 'No, I don't think you do,' he said dully, stepping back. 'It—I—It seems I've made a mistake,' his voice was stiltedly polite. 'I'm sorry.' He turned on his heel and walked to his own office farther down the corridor.

'Gideon . . .!'

Thank heaven he didn't hear her aching groan, or see the desperation in her face as he closed the door behind him. She wouldn't be bothered by him again, that much had been obvious.

She couldn't even understand why he had pursued the subject, she must have made her feelings towards him very plain over the weekend. Besides, now that she knew the truth it was a rather pointless exercise, wasn't it?

The rest of the day passed in a numbed haze for Laura, although from the sympathetic looks she received the news that she was no longer seeing Gideon had already spread through the company.

'It wasn't anything I did, was it?' Nigel asked anxiously when he gave her a lift home that evening.

The two of them had been leaving the building at the same time, and because she didn't feel in the mood to face the journey on the bus she readily accepted Nigel's offer of a lift. The fact that Gideon had travelled down with her in the lift, albeit with the curious Janice, might have encouraged her to accept the offer; Gideon's expression was thunderous.

With a curt nod of his head in their direction as a gesture of goodnight he had strode out through the double glass doors without a backward glance, getting into the waiting Jaguar and driving off.

'Laura?' Nigel prompted.

They were almost at her home, and she hadn't so much as spoken to him, let alone answered his question! The poor man didn't deserve such rude behaviour. 'No, it wasn't anything you did,' she assured him.

'You're sure?' He still seemed anxious.

'Very sure.'

'Only I think I was a little the worse for drink——'

'A little!' She smiled for what seemed the first time today—and probably was!

Nigel pulled a face. 'I can usually take my drink. It's just that I'd been watching you all evening, the way you kept glancing at the door every couple of seconds to see if Gideon had arrived.'

'I didn't——'

'You did, Laura,' he sighed. 'And when he did finally arrive your face lit up like—well, your pleasure on seeing him was obvious. It was damned annoying. I couldn't resist hitting out at him.'

Laura looked down at her hands, biting her bottom lip. 'I'm sorry.'

'It isn't your fault,' he touched one of her hands. 'Why look at me when you have Gideon interested in you?'

'Had,' she corrected softly. 'He isn't now, and I'm not interested in him either.'

'Laura——'

'It's the truth, Nigel,' she said brightly. 'And to prove it I'll invite you to dinner. Cooked by my own fair hands.' She looked at him expectantly.

'I'd like to, but——'

'I'm sorry,' she said stiltedly, 'that was presumptuous of me.' She gave a jerky smile. 'It looks as if I'm only inviting you because I'm no longer seeing Gideon.'

'That isn't the reason I'm refusing.' Nigel parked the car outside her home, turning in his seat to look at her. 'I have a previous engagement this evening, a family commitment.'

'Then of course——'

'I always visit my mother-in-law once a week,' he interrupted, his gaze holding hers steadily.

Laura gasped, paling. 'I didn't know—No one told me—You're married,' she finished dully.

'No, I'm not,' he shook his head, smiling. 'I'm divorced. Quite amicably, I might add, hence my visits to my mother-in-law.'

'I see.' But she didn't really. No one had ever mentioned Nigel being married, although the recent occurrence of her involvement with Gideon had meant no one at work talked of anything else. 'I—Do you have any children?'

'No,' Nigel's smile deepened. 'It's really all right,

Laura. Tracy and I parted the best of friends. I'm even friends with her second husband, we go fishing together.' He shrugged. 'Tracy and I were still in our teens when we married, too young to know what we were doing. When the marriage fell apart a couple of years later I don't think either of us was surprised. We just outgrew each other. It happens that way sometimes.'

'Yes. I—well, I-I'd better go in now,' she gave him a bright smile. 'Thanks for the lift.'

Nigel's hand on her arm stopped her getting out of the car. 'If you could make the dinner invitation for tomorrow night then I'd gladly accept.' He looked at her questioningly, almost warily.

'If you're sure . . .?'

'I am,' he said firmly. 'Well?'

'Tomorrow would be fine,' she confirmed eagerly. *Any* night would be fine! Now that she was no longer seeing Gideon all her evenings were free.

'Does it bother you—about Tracy and me, I mean?' Nigel frowned.

Laura blinked dazedly. 'Bother me?'

He nodded. 'It does some women, especially as I'm still friends with both Tracy and her mother.'

'Well, it doesn't bother me,' she smiled. 'In fact, I think it's rather nice.'

'So do I,' he grinned. 'And instead of you cooking me a meal tomorrow I insist on taking you out. After working all day cooking a meal is the last thing you'll feel like doing.'

'I don't mind——'

'I really do insist,' Nigel said firmly. 'Eight o'clock all right?'

'Lovely,' she nodded.

Over the next couple of weeks Laura saw a lot of Nigel. He proved to be a pleasant, undemanding companion, his goodnight kisses not exactly nerve-shattering, but pleasant nonetheless. And her growing friendship with him helped to take her mind off Gideon, who seemed more distant from people than ever.

At work she was able to treat him with the cold politeness due to any employer, and only she knew of the bitter tears she shed for him night after night. Their break-up, like their romance, was a nine-day wonder, and her friendship with Nigel now became the main topic of conversation. Going out with Nigel was a much safer relationship emotionally, and while neither of them seemed to be madly in love with the other they did have a good time together.

Her mother met him and liked him, although she couldn't understand Laura's preferring him to Gideon.

'There's just no comparison,' she dismissed scathingly three weeks later as Laura prepared for yet another date with Nigel.

'Exactly,' she acknowledged, straightening the skirt of the figure-hugging dark green dress she wore, her hair a deep auburn against its dark shade, her eyes emerald green.

'Exactly—what?' her mother sighed. 'If you would only talk about it——'

'There's nothing to talk about——'

'Don't tell me that again, Laura,' her mother snapped. 'I've listened to the same story for almost a month now, and I know that it isn't true. I hear you crying yourself to sleep every night,' she revealed with a frown. 'And that isn't because of "nothing".'

Delicate colour flooded Laura's cheeks. 'I didn't realise—I thought——'

'You thought I couldn't hear you,' her mother finished gently. 'And ordinarily I wouldn't have. But I haven't been sleeping too well myself lately——'

'Because of Mr Courtney,' Laura teased.

'Yes,' she revealed with a blush of her own. 'He's so impetuous——'

'Oh, Mum, he isn't!' She laughed at the description. 'I've seen him in action, and he never does anything that isn't completely thought out and planned to the last detail.'

Her mother looked stunned. 'You mean he means it about wanting to marry me, now, right away?'

Laura sobered. 'If that's what he's said, then yes, he means it.'

'Oh goodness . . .' Her mother sank down on to the bed, her expression dazed.

'Don't you want to marry him?' Laura asked softly.

'Oh yes—I mean, no. I—I don't know,' she blushed coyly. 'Don't you think I'm a little old to be thinking of marrying again, of changing my whole life style?'

'Not if you love him. Do you?'

'I—People of my age don't fall in love!'

'Don't be silly,' Laura chided, dismayed by this revelation for her own sake, but happy for her mother. James Courtney had obviously done a good job of sweeping her off her feet! 'You can fall in love when you're eighty.'

'I hope not!' her mother grimaced.

'You haven't answered my question,' Laura prompted, knowing the answer already. Her mother walked about with a permanent glow these days, and James Courtney wasn't the bear he had always been either, his new mellow attitude surprising a lot of people, including Laura. He wasn't the old James Courtney at all.

'I can't be——'

'Mum!'

'Well . . . I like him a lot,' Mrs Jamieson compromised. 'But marriage . . .! I need more time.'

'And Mr Courtney isn't willing to give it to you,' Laura guessed dryly.

'No,' her mother agreed with a sigh. 'He keeps pressing me for an answer!'

'Then give him one—say yes.'

'But you——'

'Are not important when it comes to your happiness.' And James Courtney did make her mother happy, she had known that from the first.

'Martin——'

Her brother had returned to America over two weeks ago, still ignorant of the fact that their mother was seeing James Courtney. 'He isn't important either,' Laura insisted. 'Goodness, do you think he's going to ask your permission to get married?'

'No, I know he isn't. But I am your mother——'

'Which is how I know how deserving you are of happiness, of a happy marriage. You and Dad weren't suited, not in any way.' Laura had always known of the friction her father's career had caused in the marriage. Her mother hated the long separations, and her father hated the long shore-leave, and so there had been constant arguing on the subject, arguments that even as a child Laura had sensed.

'And you think James and I are any more suited?' her mother scorned. 'I'm no more suited to being the wife of a millionaire than I was to be the wife of a sailor.'

'Most women wouldn't find Mr Courtney's money a drawback,' Laura teased.

'Most women don't love him like I—I mean——'

'You mean you love him,' Laura smiled. 'And if you don't accept his proposal then I'll do it for you. He——' she broke off as the doorbell rang. 'That will probably be Nigel.'

'Or James,' her mother corrected.

'Eager for his answer,' Laura grinned.

'Probably,' her mother answered ruefully. 'Could you answer the door while I go and get ready.'

It was James Courtney, looking very handsome and distinguished, as usual. Although he was more disparaging about Laura's appearance.

'You look like a ghost,' he barked critically, sitting himself in the chair opposite her as they waited for her mother.

Laura pulled a face at him. 'Taking up your stepfather duties already?' she taunted.

He gave a boyish flush. 'Your mother told you, then?'

'Oh yes,' she nodded.

'And?' It was almost a challenge.

'I approve.'

'You do?' He seemed surprised.

'I do,' Laura nodded with a smile.

'Well, I'll be damned!'

She was grinning openly now. 'Were you expecting opposition?'

'To tell you the truth I had no idea what your reaction would be,' he admitted ruefully.

'And you didn't care either,' she laughed.

'Oh, I cared, for your mother's sake. You're very important to her, you and your brother. She would never do anything of which you disapproved.' His expression darkened at her frown. 'What is it?' he demanded.

'*I* approve,' she said slowly. 'But Martin——'

'Won't?'

'Probably not.'

'I'm not going to lose your mother, not for any reason,' James growled. 'She's the best thing that's happened to me for years. After my heart attack——'

'I didn't know,' Laura frowned.

'It was years ago,' he dismissed. 'I haven't had any trouble from it since then. And as long as I don't overtax myself I shouldn't have any more attacks. Don't worry, I'm not going to leave your mother a widow as soon as we're married. I wouldn't even think of marrying her if I thought I was going to die. She deserves better than that.'

His words showed he knew of the unhappiness of her

mother's first marriage, and only her mother could have told him of that. Which only went to prove how much her mother did love this man.

'Yes,' Laura agreed huskily.

'I could make her happy,' James growled.

'I'm sure you could,' she nodded.

'But you still don't think your brother will agree?'

'No,' she sighed. She had an awful feeling that when Martin was told the news he would blurt out his past relationship with James's daughter. And what would that do for James's heart condition?

James frowned angrily. 'Well, he'll damn well have to put up with it,' he snapped. 'I won't take no for an answer. I'm certainly not going to let Martin ruin things for us.'

'I hope you're right.'

'I will be.' Once again he looked at her critically. 'Going out, are you?'

'Why?' she asked innocently. 'Do you intend seducing my mother while I'm gone?'

James gave a loud shout of laughter. 'You're a cheeky little madam,' he chuckled.

'Does that mean seduction isn't on the programme?'

'I may try that if all else fails to get a positive response to my marriage proposal.' He was suddenly serious. 'I do want your mother in that way,' he told her candidly. 'I want her in every way a man in love can want and need a woman.'

'I know,' Laura acknowledged huskily. 'And she feels the same way. Although I think she's a little shocked at herself, at her age.'

'She's just a baby!' he scoffed. 'How much longer to you intend putting Gideon through hell?' he pounced suddenly, pinpointing her with his icy blue stare.

'I—You—I——' He had caught her completely off guard, which was probably his intention!

'Well?' he prompted tersely.

'Mind your own business!' she snapped her agitation, standing up.

'It is my business. So?'

'Gideon isn't going through hell,' her eyes flashed. 'At least, not on my account.'

'And just how do you know that?'

'I know,' she said with conviction. 'Because I know Gideon better than you do.'

'Don't be ridiculous, girl,' James snapped. 'I've known Gideon——'

'In a business capacity,' she interrupted heatedly. 'You have no idea what he's really like.'

'Considering I helped bring him up I have a very good idea of what he's like,' James corrected.

'*You* brought him up?' Laura gasped, paling.

James nodded. 'Since his father died.'

'Which was when?'

'About twenty years ago. Gideon was about sixteen at the time.'

'I—I see.' So Gideon had almost grown up with Felicity. How strange! And how could Gideon have so betrayed James's love and trust, marrying the beloved daughter of the man who had done so much for him, even knowing he didn't love her? Her feelings towards Gideon hardened even more. 'Then you obviously do know what sort of a man he is.' Her tone was scornful.

'Yes, I know,' James rasped harshly. 'And so would you if you had any sense at all. I want to see Gideon happy, and for some reason,' his expression mocked, '*you* seem to make him happy. Jealously happy, but nonetheless happy.'

Laura turned away. 'You don't know what you're talking about.'

'I know, girl,' he snapped impatiently. 'And so would you if you've looked at Gideon lately.'

Looked at him! Heavens, she couldn't seem to do anything else! 'He seems the same as he's always been,' she dismissed.

James's eyes were narrowed. 'Which is?'

'Cold and calculating!'

His mouth twisted in disgust. 'You're a fool, girl.'

Her mother entered the room at that moment, looking warily at the two set faces in front of her. 'Is there anything wrong?'

James controlled his anger with effort, turning to smile at her. 'No, of course not, Joan. Is there, Laura?' his tone was warning.

'No,' she gave a bright smile. 'I was just telling Mr Courtney how lucky he is to be having you for his wife.'

Her mother blushed, looking coyly at James. 'I think you're a little premature, Laura.'

'Not at all, Joan,' James said dismissively. 'I don't intend taking no for an answer. And the wedding is going to be soon.'

'James——'

'Soon, Joan,' he repeated firmly.

'But I——'

'Oh, give in gracefully, Mum,' Laura grinned, enjoying seeing her mother being dominated in this way. And her mother seemed to like it too, having had too much responsibility alone for too long, relieved to be able at last to share some of her worries. 'Just think, Mr Courtney——'

'James,' he corrected gruffly. 'Or Dad if you can manage it.'

'Well, really,' her mother began indignantly. 'I——'

'I think James for now,' Laura ignored her mother's outburst. 'Maybe Dad later.'

'But——'

'That's fine by me,' James nodded, also ignoring her mother. 'You were saying?' he prompted Laura.

She grinned teasingly. 'I was just going to point out the pleasure of having me as a stepdaughter.'

'I knew from the first that we were going to be related in some way. I had a different relationship in mind, but then I can't have everything,' he added infuriatingly.

'You certainly can't,' Laura told him waspishly, knowing that he had approved of her going out with Gideon. If he knew the reason for Gideon's interest he might feel less kindly disposed towards him. 'That will be my date,' she said with relief as the doorbell rang.

'Young Jennings, isn't it?' James asked curtly.

'Yes,' she confirmed abruptly.

'Nice enough chap——'

'I'm sure he'll be glad of your approval.' Her mouth twisted mockingly.

James quirked a taunting eyebrow over light blue eyes. 'I didn't say I approved, I said he was a nice enough chap. But not for you.'

'I——'

'Go and answer the door, girl,' he ordered gruffly. 'He sounds impatient to see you. But think over what I said about Gideon.'

'I have no intention of giving him a single thought,' she snapped. 'Now, if you'll excuse me . . .'

James made no further attempt to prevent her departure, although she had the awful feeling that once he was her stepfather he might have a lot more to say on the subject of Gideon!

CHAPTER EIGHT

No doubt James would have been pleased to know Laura's relationship with Nigel had stagnated. And she knew it was mainly her fault. She kept their conversation light, their goodnight kisses even lighter. That Nigel was aware of her deliberate restraint in their friendship she knew, and she liked him all the more for respecting the hurt she had suffered at Gideon's cruel hands.

It had been impossible to hide it from Nigel, to keep up the pretence she presented to everyone else, including Gideon himself. Knowing his reasons for going out with her he was the person she most had to convince that he had meant nothing to her. She felt sure she had succeeded.

The news of her mother's pending marriage to James Courtney spread through the company like wildfire, and James' benign attitude was at last explained. By Monday evening it seemed that everyone knew, and most were congratulating *her*, as if she had pulled off a really clever move. Maybe to the outsider it looked as if she had—after all, she hadn't got Gideon, but her mother was marrying James. She wondered if that was the way Gideon would see it too.

He had been out of the office all morning, although she had seen him walk past the office towards late afternoon, glancing to neither left nor right, his expression as remote as usual.

He must know that the wedding was to take place on Saturday, James was sure to have told him by now. The speed with which the marriage was to take place came as no surprise to Laura, although her mother still seemed a bit dazed by it all. But Laura had a feeling her warning about Martin might have something to do with James's haste. Once her mother was married to James Martin wouldn't be able to cause any lasting damage. At least, she hoped he wouldn't. She had no intention of telling him about the wedding until it was over, telling her mother that he would never be able to get the time off so soon after his last holiday.

'Wait for me,' James instructed her at five o'clock as Dorothy and Janice prepared to leave. 'I have something I want to discuss with you.'

Laura accepted the other girls' cheery goodnights, feeling somewhat awkward about her sudden change of relationship to James. It seemed he was aware of the awkwardness too.

'I can't have my stepdaughter as my junior secretary,' he scowled at her across his desk.

Laura stood in front of him, thinking in amazement that it had only been a few weeks ago that she had felt shy and uncomfortable about even entering his office, and now he was going to be her stepfather! It seemed incredible.

'What would you suggest?' she teased. 'That I hand in my notice?'

'Hell, no!' he took her seriously. 'I had promotion in mind.' He eyed her questioningly.

All humour left her. 'The fact that you're marrying my mother does not entitle me to any favouritism——'

'Of course it does,' he dismissed scathingly. 'You'll be my daughter, and as such you should be higher up in the company than my junior secretary.'

'Higher? But Dorothy has been here years, and I——'

'Good God, girl, I'm not thinking of dismissing Dorothy!' He sounded scandalised. 'I'm too old to be changing my secretary now. Dorothy knows all my little quirks—Stop laughing, Laura,' he snapped. 'At my age

I'm allowed to have quirks.'

'Sorry,' she still chuckled. 'But if I'm not to replace Dorothy, what am I to do?'

'Replace Diane Holland,' James stated calmly.

Laura paled, clutching the back of the chair for support, slowly moving forward to lower herself down on to its hardness. 'I—You have to be joking,' she croaked at last.

'Ever known me to joke?' he taunted.

'I—No,' she admitted lamely. 'But I don't want to be Gideon's secretary.' Once upon a time she couldn't have thought of anything she would enjoy more, but not now, *not now*!

James shifted some papers about on his desk. 'I'm not asking you, Laura, I'm telling you—if you want to remain in employment at Courtneys,' he added warningly.

Laura swallowed hard. 'But *Gideon's* secretary...!

He raised a querying eyebrow. 'Is there any reason for the emphasis?'

Her eyes flashed deeply green. 'You know there is!'

'Do I?'

'Yes!' she hissed. 'I can't work with Gideon. I can't!'

'You wouldn't be working with him, but *for* him.'

'All the more reason——!' She stood up. 'I think I would rather leave.' She turned and walked to the door.

'And how do you think your mother will feel about that?' James softly taunted.

Laura turned angrily. 'That isn't fair!'

'I don't think anyone's ever accused me of being that,' his mouth quirked.

'Oh, please don't do this to me,' she pleaded huskily. 'If I take Diane's place what will she do? Surely you can see——'

'Diane Holland is leaving us, sadly. Her husband is setting up in business for himself, and Diane has decided to help him.'

'But Janice——'

'Would rather stay with me,' he told her with quiet satisfaction.

'Oh, but—There must be other girls in the company who could do the job better than me——'

'I'm not offering it to them,' James drawled. 'I'm offering it to you. Well?'

'Does Gid—Does Mr Maitland know about this?' She blushed at her slip, always using the formality when she was at work, even when talking to James.

'Yes, *Gideon* knows about it,' he taunted her.

She swallowed hard. 'And?'

'And what?' James quirked an infuriating eyebrow.

'I'm sure he can't be any more favourably disposed to the idea than I am,' she snapped.

James's expression hardened. 'I am still the chairman of this company,' he told her icily. 'And as such I still make the decisions.'

'And you've decided I'm to be Gideon's secretary,' she said dully.

'Exactly,' he confirmed with satisfaction.

'Why?'

'I thought I'd just explained that Diane——'

'Not that bit,' Laura interrupted impatiently. 'Why do *you* want me to work wi—for Gideon?'

'You're a damned good secretary——'

'The real reason,' she sighed.

He nodded. 'Okay. If the two of you work closely together all day you may, and I emphasise the may, just come to your senses. Both of you.'

'By "coming to our senses" you mean we might become—friends again?' Laura said dryly.

'Yes.'

'No chance,' she told him with certainty.

'No?'

'No!'

'We'll see.' His mouth twisted.

Laura licked her lips nervously. 'Just out of curiosity, what was Gideon's reaction?'

From the quirk of his often stern mouth he obviously found her forced casualness amusing. 'What do you think it was?' he mocked.

She gave an impatient sigh. 'You tell me.'

'It was the same as yours.'

She went even paler. 'He doesn't want to work with me either?'

'No.'

'Then don't do this to us!' she groaned, hoping he couldn't see the pain his words had caused, but very much afraid his sharp gaze had picked up her every emotion.

James stood up in preparation for ending the conversation. 'I've already done it. Starting tomorrow you'll be working alongside Diane learning all there is to know about her job. She leaves at the end of the month.' He picked up his briefcase. 'Can I give you a lift home?'

'No, thank you.'

'Jennings again?' he frowned.

'Bus,' she mocked. 'I'm working until six this evening— six-fifteen now,' she added pointedly at this unscheduled talk with him.

James nodded. 'Perhaps I'll see you later, then.'

Considering he had been at her home every day for the past four weeks she didn't even bother to answer this statement, but went back to her desk to complete the work that it now appeared would be her last as James's junior secretary.

She couldn't leave Courtneys, James knew that. It would upset her mother, and right now she didn't want to do that. At the moment her mother was the happiest she had ever seen her, and if working with Gideon was going to continue that happiness then that was what she would do. Her mother had had a hard life up to now, bringing up two children more or less single-handed, and now she was going to be the pampered one, the adored wife of a rich man. And she wouldn't do anything to jeopardise that.

The fact that James knew of her reluctance to distress her mother at this time increased her anger towards him. He was a wily, interfering man, and she had the feeling she would have more trouble from him during the next few months. If only she could make him understand that she and Gideon were finished, for good. He was such a——

'Laura . . .'

She raised a white face at the sound of that husky voice, looking straight at Gideon, his features taut and drawn. 'Gideon . . .' She was too startled to use formality.

The office staff at Courtneys often did overtime, but she had thought she was the only person left on the top floor. It seemed she was wrong, there was only her and *Gideon* on the top floor. If there was anyone else in the building it wasn't apparent, the two of them were surrounded by an eerie silence, the rush and bustle of the day seeming almost not to have happened.

He came into the room and closed the door behind him, adding to the intimacy of the situation.

To see Gideon now, alone here like this, was the last thing she wanted. While she was able to view him from a distance, surrounded by other people, she was at least able to act businesslike, if not exactly friendly. On a one-to-one basis she felt far from capable of coping with the situation, especially with Gideon looking so vitally attractive, his male sensuality working on her like a magnet. He looked so handsome in the dark three-piece suit, so dangerously attractive she instantly felt threatened.

She forced a calm expression to her face. 'Can I do anything for you, Mr Maitland?' she asked stiltedly.

His mouth twisted. 'I think you know the answer to

that,' he drawled mockingly.

Laura blushed—as he had intended she should, damn him! 'I meant in my official capacity,' she flashed. 'As your new secretary.'

'Ah,' he perched on the side of her desk, idly picking up the paperweight and studying it, 'so James has told you.'

'Yes.' She was unnerved by his closeness, wished herself anywhere but alone with him here.

Gideon quirked an eyebrow at her. 'Any comment?'

'None,' she answered stiffly. 'You?'

'No.'

'Then it's all settled.' She shifted some papers about on her desk, wishing he would leave.

Gideon halted her movements, his hand firm on hers. 'I can ask James to make other arrangements if you would prefer it,' he said huskily.

Laura looked at the way one of his hands covered both of hers, a strong, dependable hand that knew how to caress her to abandonment, a hand that knew her more intimately than any other. The thought made her blush, unable to look up at Gideon in case he should see the hunger in her face, the longing to be in his arms that she couldn't deny.

'As I said, it's settled,' she mumbled.

'It can be unsettled.'

'If you would rather I didn't——' She broke off, having looked up in anger, at once mesmerised by his face only inches from her own. She shouldn't have looked up, shouldn't have let him see the reaction his hand touching her was invoking. 'If you would rather I—rather I didn't become your—your secretary,' she stuttered and stumbled over the words, feeling herself inevitably drawn towards him, as his hands on her elbows drew her nearer and nearer. 'I—I'm sure James would—that he would respect your wishes,' she added lamely.

'Oh, I want you for my secretary, Laura,' Gideon told her softly, his mouth only inches away from hers now. 'But I want more, so much more. Laura . . .!' he groaned before his mouth claimed hers.

She forgot the past, forgot the bitterness of their parting, forgot everything but the wild sensations coursing through her body. After she had thought never to be in Gideon's arms again it was exquisite torture to be here with him like this, although perhaps it was as well that they weren't in a more private place. She had no idea how she was to stop the soul-destroying kisses, or whether, in fact, she wanted them to end.

Gideon certainly seemed to have no such inhibitions, as he stood up to mould her body to his, letting her know by the pulsating hardness of his body just how deeply he was aroused.

His hands ran intimately over her body, heatedly undoing several of the buttons on her blouse to smooth the silky material from her shoulders, his lips lowering to the milky-white flesh there.

Laura gasped as one of his hands captured her breast, caressing the hardened tip even through the gossamer of her bra, and her reaction was instantaneous.

'Touch me, Laura,' he groaned. 'For God's sake touch me!'

'Gideon——'

'I need you, Laura,' he moaned, moving her hands to his waistcoat, helping her undo the half a dozen buttons before pressing her hand against his shirt. 'Undo that too,' he muttered against her throat. 'Touch my flesh, Laura,' he seemed to shudder just at the thought of it.

She fumbled with the buttons, but Gideon made no effort to help her, his attention all on the breasts he had bared to his caressing tongue, groaning in his throat as he at last felt her hands entangle in the dark, silky hair on his chest, clutching at his taut waist as he continued his caressing of her nipples.

It was a complete explosion of the senses between them, the demands of their bodies having taken over, their naked torsos seared together in heated desire, their mouths fused together in a ritual as old as time itself.

'I want you!' Gideon raised his head to gasp, his eyes glowing like black coals in his pale face. 'Laura, I want you now.'

'Not here. And not now,' she cried her dismay. 'I—I couldn't, not here!'

He buttoned her blouse with unsteady fingers. 'Come with me,' he held her hand in his as he waited for her answer.

'I can't!' she groaned, closing her eyes to shut out the beautiful sight of him, wishing this were all a terrible dream. 'I—Please,' she frantically buttoned his shirt for him. 'It was a mistake. I—I didn't—I don't know what happened,' she admitted miserably. 'I didn't mean for it to happen,' she added lamely.

She was so ashamed, so embarrassed she couldn't even look at Gideon. And her behaviour just now had been disloyal to Nigel and the friendship he had shown her the last few weeks—a friendship she knew she could no longer take advantage of. If she could act this way with Gideon then she had no right to go out with Nigel.

Gideon's expression darkened as he moved forcefully away from her. 'You didn't *mean* for it to happen!' he bit out savagely. 'Then what the hell *did* you *mean*?'

Laura was very pale. 'I don't know,' she groaned her misery.

'God, Laura, were you *playing* with me?' he rasped.

'No!' she raised startled eyes. 'Of course not. You wanted it as much as I did,' she accused indignantly.

'I didn't want *it*, I wanted you,' he told her harshly. 'I always have.'

Laura's mouth twisted bitterly. 'Always, Gideon? Or

just since you found out Martin is my brother?'

'Of course I knew Martin was your brother——'

'Of course you did,' she agreed scornfully.

'But it made no difference,' he finished grimly.

'No difference to what?' she gasped.

'To the fact that I was attracted to you, that I wanted you to go out with me.'

Laura shook her head in dismissal. 'You don't expect me to believe all this, do you?'

A pulse beat erratically at his jawline. 'It's obvious you don't.'

'No, I don't,' she snapped.

He gave a sigh of defeat. 'Then I'm sorry, sorrier than you'll ever know. Goodnight, Laura.' He was once again the remote employer.

'Goodnight—Mr Maitland. I won't be late in the morning,' she added as a reminder, to herself as much as anyone, that she would be working for Gideon from now on.

'I'm sure of it.' His mouth twisted before he moved to the door. 'And just for the record, Laura, I admire your spirit.'

'Just for the record, with James as a stepfather, I think I'm going to need it,' she told him ruefully, knowing that the two of them couldn't work together in this strained atmosphere. A compromise would have to be reached, and tonight, before they had the keen audience of Diane Holland. But how could they come to a compromise after the passion they had just shared?

'If he gets too much for you,' Gideon seemed to sense her desire for, if not friendship, then at least a truce, 'just let me know. I'm years ahead of you when it comes to handling James.'

'So he told me.' She was aware that they were walking on fragile ice, that an argument could break open again at any moment if either of them said a word out of place.

And yet they had to strive for this politeness if they were to work together at all.

Gideon raised his eyebrows. 'He told you that he helped bring me up?'

'Yes.'

His expression was guarded now. 'Did he tell you anything else?'

'Should he have done?' she frowned.

Gideon shrugged, buttoning his waistcoat, looking now as if that heated encounter had never taken place. 'James seems to be playing chief matchmaker between us at the moment——'

'Not with you too!' she groaned, her face coloured with embarrassment.

'Afraid so,' he gave a rueful nod.

'I'm sorry. I——'

'Hey, it isn't your fault,' he chided softly. 'James has an idea in his head, and it will take a bomb to shift it. Your brother——' he suddenly changed the subject, catching her off guard.

'What about him?' she asked defensively.

'Will he be at the wedding?'

'No,' she answered with relief; she had been tense as she waited to see what he had to say about Martin. 'It's too soon after his last holiday.' Besides which, he knew nothing about the wedding, and wouldn't until their mother was safely married to James!

'In that case, perhaps I could take you?'

Laura gave him a sharp look, searching his calm grey eyes. 'Why should you want to do that?'

'You won't have a partner——'

Oh God, he felt sorry for her! 'Nigel will be with me,' she told him stiltedly.

A shutter seemed to come down over his features, his mouth a thin line, his eyes glacial. 'Of course, you're still seeing him,' he rasped.

'Of course. And how is Mrs Harlow?'

Impatience flickered in his dark grey eyes. 'Laura——'

'She's well, I hope?'

'Yes. But——'

'Good,' she interrupted dismissively, turning pointedly to the work on her desk. 'If you'll excuse me, I have to get this finished. I have a date tonight.'

Gideon was every inch the haughty executive now, only his tousled dark hair reminding her of the way she had feverishly run her hands through it minutes earlier. 'I'm sorry I delayed you.'

'That's perfectly all right, Mr Maitland,' she replied primly, no longer looking at him but at her work.

He thrust her chin up savagely. 'You'll call me Gideon in front of Diane,' he told her forcefully. 'Save your antipathy for when we're alone.'

She wrenched out of his grasp. 'I'll do that,' she said fiercely, glaring at him.

'God, Laura, you—Oh, hell!' He threw the door open, slamming out of the room.

Laura collapsed exhaustedly on to the desk. Working with Gideon just couldn't work out, it couldn't! Because she still loved him, no matter how he had used her!

Her mother was predictably ecstatic about her promotion to Gideon's secretary, sure that James had only Laura's best interests at heart. Laura wished she could feel as confident of that!

'It *is* a good promotion,' Nigel told her later that evening. The two of them were alone at Laura's home, her mother and James having gone to the theatre for the evening, a welcome break for them after the rush and bustle of the wedding arrangements.

Laura had been too weary and dispirited to feel interested in going out herself, although Nigel had wanted to take her out to celebrate her promotion. She preferred to spend the evening at home—after all, what did she really have to celebrate?

'A bit embarrassing, maybe,' he continued thoughtfully.

'A bit!' she scorned. 'It's going to be awful.'

'Is Gideon aware of the arrangement?'

'Yes,' she sighed, pushing her hair back irritably from her face.

Nigel raised his eyebrows. 'I take it he has no objections?'

'He didn't mention any.'

'Hm,' Nigel said slowly.

'Hm, what?' she asked sharply, frowning heavily.

'Just hm. Any more coffee going?' he changed the subject.

'Hm, what, Nigel?' Laura persisted, not willing to let the subject go.

'Does that mean there's no coffee?'

'Nigel!' She had provided him with dinner, and now they were in the lounge enjoying their coffee together. 'I'll get you another drink in a moment. Now what did you mean?'

'Well, Gideon didn't object to having you as his secretary, did he?'

'Not to my face,' although she remembered James said he had been reluctant.

'I wonder why.'

'It isn't his place to object——'

'Of course it is,' Nigel snorted. 'Hey, I'm the Personnel Officer, and believe me, if Gideon didn't want you he wouldn't have you.'

'James——'

'Certainly doesn't rule Gideon. He never has.'

Laura frowned her puzzlement. Why *had* Gideon accepted her as his secretary? She didn't want to probe the reasons just now, just as she didn't want to think of his desire earlier this evening, his clamouring to make love to her.

'Does it matter?' she dismissed.

Nigel frowned heavily. 'I think so. You never did tell me why the two of you broke up.'

'It wasn't important.' She evaded his eyes.

'If it isn't important why won't you talk about it?'

'Nigel!' she sighed. 'Please, let's just drop the subject.'

'I don't think I can.' He sat forward in his seat. 'You see, Laura, I like you a lot myself, and while you still have this hang-up for Gideon——'

'It isn't a hang-up!' she flushed.

'No,' he sighed acknowledgement of the fact. 'It's more than that, much more. I have to be honest with you, Laura, and tell you that I've been thinking of marrying again.'

'Oh.' Her heart sank. 'I—Do I know her?'

'You did,' he gave a rueful smile, taking her hand in his. 'It just hasn't worked out.'

She licked her lips nervously. 'You mean—me?' She hardly dared voice the thought.

'Don't look so surprised,' he chuckled. 'You're beautiful, young, fun to be with, and you seem to like kids.'

'Er—yes,' she frowned.

'And most important of all, I like you, more than like you.' He shrugged. 'I'm not getting any younger, and I would like to marry and have children before I get much older. Unfortunately I seem to have become fond of a girl who's in love with another man.'

'No!'

'Laura,' he said reprovingly. 'You love Gideon. And I happen to think he loves you too.'

'Why does everyone——' She broke off, biting her bottom lip. 'He doesn't love me,' she said stubbornly.

'Who else thinks he does?' Nigel correctly guessed her unfinished sentence.

'No one. I'm sorry things haven't worked out, Nigel. I've enjoyed going out with you, and——'

'Who else, Laura?' he persisted.

'It doesn't matter——'

'Your future stepfather, right?'

Her eyes widened. 'How did you know?'

'Maybe his glowering attitude towards me lately.' He grinned. 'I don't think I've ever been his favourite person, but just lately . . . Well, something's been bothering him. He wants you for Gideon too?'

'Too?' she frowned.

'Gideon seems to want you for Gideon as well,' he explained ruefully. 'His attitude towards me has been even more chilling than James's.'

'You're imagining things——'

'No,' Nigel shook his head, squeezing her hand. 'I want to stay your friend, Laura, but as far as anything else goes I think we should call it a day You're never likely to patch things up with Gideon with me around.'

'We're never likely to do that anyway,' she said bitterly. 'You see, we—we weren't the only people involved.'

Nigel gave a disbelieving frown. 'Gideon was seeing another woman?'

'Among other things,' she nodded.

'When?'

'What do you mean, when?'

'Well, as I remember it, you saw each other almost every night during the time you were going together.'

'Except when he went to Manchester——'

'Where he worked constantly. The unions were being difficult, and the meetings went on almost day and night. Gideon barely slept, let alone saw another woman.'

'It wasn't only that.' She could hardly tell him that the 'other woman' actually lived in Gideon's house with him.

'Can I take a guess?' Nigel quirked an eyebrow. 'Martin, right?'

Laura gasped. 'How did you know—I mean, whatever gave you that idea?' she strove for casualness.

'Martin and I were friends when he worked at Courtneys,' Nigel revealed.

'Then you know—you know about—about——'

'Felicity? Yes,' he nodded. 'I was one of the few who did. Gideon was another one.'

'Yes,' Laura agreed heavily.

'He could hardly help his wife's affair with your brother,' Nigel pointed out gently.

'He could help punishing me for it!' She stood up agitatedly. 'I'm sorry, Nigel, I didn't mean to shout.'

'That's okay. But I'm not understanding any of this,' he shook his head. 'Just what have you dreamt up in that confused mind of yours?'

'I'm not confused. And I didn't dream it up. Martin accused Gideon of using me to get back at him——'

'And what did Gideon do?'

'He denied it, of course,' she recalled impatiently. 'But then he would, wouldn't he?'

'Would he?'

'Well—yes.'

'Why?'

'Because—well, because——'

He shook his head. 'You haven't been thinking straight, Laura. And Martin was acting out of anger and pain. If Gideon had been going out with you as a means of revenge on his wife's lover—God, how melodramatic that sounds! If that were his reason for going out with you don't you think he would have enjoyed telling Martin that?'

'I——'

'Reason it out, Laura,' he encouraged. 'If he wanted revenge he would have taken it then.'

'But he didn't . . .'

'No, he didn't. Because Felicity and Martin have nothing to do with the two of you. They were the past, and Gideon has buried the past. He wasn't very happy in those days——'

'Then he shouldn't have married a woman he didn't love!' She tried to keep her anger against him, although each word Nigel spoke seemed to be breaking down her defences. 'He just wanted to get his hands on Courtneys——'

'He didn't have to marry Felicity for that.' Nigel frowned. 'Who told you all this? Martin?' he asked disbelievingly. 'God, he must be bitter!'

'And shouldn't he be?' Laura was indignant on her brother's behalf.

'Maybe,' Nigel conceded. 'But not so bitter that he should try and ruin your life too. It isn't true that Gideon needed to marry Felicity to get control of Courtneys. Gideon's father was James Courtney's junior partner a long time ago, making Gideon his partner now, making Gideon the next rightful chairman of Courtneys.'

Laura frowned. 'I didn't know that.' Although it would explain why James had taken over Gideon's care when his father had died.

'There seems to be a lot you don't know.' Nigel stood up. 'And I don't think I'm the one to tell you. I think you know who is?'

She swallowed hard. 'Gideon?'

He nodded. 'I'm sure he must have tried to explain to you.' He saw her blush. 'Yes, I thought so. Maybe now is the time to listen, hmm?'

'I—I don't know.' She twisted her hands together. 'What if you're wrong?'

'What have you got to lose?'

Only her pride. And she was beginning to think that wasn't worth much.

Nigel pulled on his jacket. 'Call him. It's only eleven o'clock. And the way Gideon's been looking lately I doubt he's asleep.' He bent down and kissed her lightly on the cheek. 'Don't invite me to the wedding, I'm a bad loser.'

'Liar,' she smiled. 'You wouldn't be doing this if you were a bad loser.'

'Maybe not,' he gave a rueful smile. 'But make the call, eh?'

'I—I'll think about it.'

'Laura!'

'I can't promise more than that,' she told him pleadingly. 'You could be wrong, you know.'

'I could,' he nodded. 'But one telephone call isn't going to hurt you.'

'I have to work with him tomorrow——'

'Take a chance, Laura,' he encouraged.

She stared at the telephone for over half an hour after Nigel had left, still undecided about whether or not she should call Gideon. She had nothing to lose, not when she had already admitted her love for him, and she had so much to gain if Nigel was right. But still she hesitated . . .

Her mother was alone when she came home. 'James has an early appointment,' she explained. 'Has Nigel gone?'

'Yes, he—he had to leave early.'

'Then why haven't you gone to bed, dear? It's almost twelve o'clock, you know.'

'Yes, I know,' Laura sighed. 'Mum, have you seen Gideon lately?'

Her mother's gaze was instantly evasive. 'A few times,' she nodded.

'And how—how does he treat you?'

She frowned. 'Treat me? I don't understand what you mean.'

'Well, is he—is he polite to you?' Laura looked at her mother searchingly.

'Of course he's polite!' She sounded surprised by such a question. 'He's always very friendly.'

'Always?' she frowned.

Her mother flushed. 'Well, James and I often take

Natalie out, so I see Gideon then. He's never been anything but polite to me.'

'But friendly with it?' Laura persisted. Surely if Gideon genuinely felt he had a grievance against her family then it would include her mother. He could be polite to her for James's sake, but he didn't have to be friendly too.

'Very friendly,' her mother nodded. 'And he always asks about you.'

Had she misjudged his motives? His open desire earlier this evening seemed to say she had.

'Thanks, Mum,' she glowed. 'I want to make a telephone call now.'

'This time of night?' her mother gasped. 'Who on earth—To Gideon?' she suddenly realised.

'Yes.'

'Then I'll go to my room,' she smiled, kissing Laura on the cheek. 'And I think you're doing the right thing, dear.'

'Let's hope so!'

Still Laura hesitated once she was alone again. It was twelve o'clock at night, much too late to be telephoning anyone. But if she didn't make the call now she probably never would, would find half a dozen reasons why she shouldn't.

To her surprise Gideon answered the telephone himself, putting her completely off guard. She would recognise his husky tones anywhere.

'I—I hope I didn't wake you,' she said tentatively.

The line seemed to crackle with tension for long timeless seconds. 'Laura?' his voice was sharp.

'Yes,' she confirmed huskily.

'Is there anything wrong? Your mother—James——'

'No they—they're both fine. I—I was just wondering— Er—Gideon, if I told you I was willing to listen now, what would you say?' The last came out in a rush, and she held her breath as she waited for his answer.

'I would say, are you sure?' he asked huskily.

'Very sure,' she answered strongly.

'Then I'm coming over. Is that all right with you?'

It was very all right with her! 'Twenty minutes?' she said breathlessly.

'Make it fifteen,' he told her before putting down the receiver.

Well, she had done it now. In fifteen minutes Gideon would be here, in this very room. What would be the outcome of their meeting?

CHAPTER NINE

By the time the doorbell rang fifteen minutes later to announce Gideon's arrival Laura had got herself into such a state of nerves she hardly knew how to face him.

She had stood anxiously at the window waiting for his car to draw up outside, running to open the door before he could ring the bell for a second time. Her mother could be asleep by now—although somehow she doubted it.

Gideon looked extremely handsome in close-fitting faded denims and a navy blue shirt, the latter partly unbuttoned down his throat to reveal the dark hair on his chest.

'Er—Hello,' she greeted shyly.

'Hello,' he returned deeply, his expression wary.

'I—Won't you come in?' She jerkily opened the door.

'Thanks.' He stepped inside and walked through to the lounge, at once dominating his surroundings.

Laura followed him nervously, running her hands down her own denim-clad thighs. What did she say now? She had asked him here, and now she didn't know what to say to him!

'I didn't wake you, did I?' she repeated the remark he hadn't answered on the telephone.

'No.' His gaze never left her flushed face.

Laura shifted uncomfortably. He could at least help her in this. But why should he? She was the one to instigate this late night meeting, he had tried to talk to her often enough in the past and she had rejected him. But that didn't make it any easier for her to talk to him now!

'Would you like a cup of coffee?' she offered.

His mouth twisted. 'No—thank you,' he added be-
latedly.

'Oh.' She looked down at the carpet, wondering where
to start.

'Was this a mistake, Laura?' he broke tersely into the
awkward silence. 'Would you like me to leave?'

'No!' she cried pleadingly, looking up into his angry
face, the grey eyes glittering with impatience. 'I don't
know where to start,' she told him miserably.

'Then I'd better help you,' he sighed. 'Can I sit down?'

'Yes—of course,' she said eagerly. 'Are you sure you
wouldn't like a cup of coffee?'

'Very sure,' he drawled, sitting down in one of the
armchairs, his long legs stretched out in front of him.
'Now, we can start with the reason you've decided to listen
to me.' His eyes were narrowed as he looked at her. 'Why
have you?'

'I just thought——'

'You did? Alone?' he asked suspiciously.

'Well . . . no. But——'

'James!' He was suddenly tense.

'No,' she shook her head frantically. 'It was Nigel.'

Puzzlement flickered across his hard features. 'Nigel
persuaded you to hear me out?' he said slowly.

She gave a rueful smile. 'I didn't need much persuad-
ing,' she admitted. 'When you kissed me earlier——'

'Let's leave that out of this, Laura,' Gideon dismissed
tersely. 'It can only cloud the issue.'

How could she leave her love out of this? If she didn't
love him so much she wouldn't have been so hurt by what
she believed to be his 'using' of her, and she wouldn't
have wanted to see him now. But Gideon was making it
clear he wasn't interested in that love. He was here to
clear up the misunderstandings of the past, and that was
all he was here for.

She bit her lip. 'Nigel believes I've been wrong about

you, about your motives.'

Gideon's mouth twisted. 'Big of him.'

'I think so,' she flashed. 'Not many men would—would—well, I think it's very big of him,' she defended.

'Perhaps,' he nodded curtly, standing up. 'I think this was a mistake after all. I have no intention of baring my soul to you in the circumstances. I hope you'll be very happy with Nigel, he's a good man.'

'Nigel . . .? But——' She watched Gideon walk to the door. 'Don't go!'

He turned angrily, his expression fierce. 'What more do you want from me, Laura. A confession of love? An admission of need?' He ran an agitated hand through his tousled dark hair. 'God knows both are true,' he added derisively. 'But if you were expecting any pleas of forgiveness on my part then you're out of luck. I have nothing to ask forgiveness for. Nothing!' He turned to leave.

'Gideon, please!' She ran to him, her hand on his arm preventing him from leaving. One look at his hard unrelenting face was enough to tell her that she had better find the right words this time or lose Gideon for ever. She wet her lips nervously. 'Gideon, you admitted to love,' God, she could hardly believe that! 'And need,' this she found even harder to believe, never imagining Gideon needing anyone. 'Well, I admit to love and need too.' She looked up at him pleadingly.

His eyes glazed over like chips of ice, his mouth firm. 'I'm sure Nigel is very happy about that.'

Temper rose within her at his lack of understanding. 'You stupid, stupid man!' she snapped angrily, facing him defiantly as his face darkened. 'I would hardly want to see you just to tell you I'm in love with Nigel.'

'Wouldn't you?' he said bitterly.

'It's you I love, *you* I need. But if you're too stupid to see that, I—Gideon!' she gasped as he swept her up against him, her feet completely off the ground. 'Gideon, put me down!'

'Never!' he growled against her ear. 'I love you, you confused, utterly adorable child. And I'm going to marry you.'

She stopped pounding on his chest to slowly look up at him, her eyes huge with wonder in her pale face. 'You— you are?'

'I am,' he told her firmly. 'Any objections, Miss Jamieson?'

'None at all, Mr Maitland,' she answered in her most efficient secretarial voice.

'Very well.' Humour lightened his eyes, the tension about his mouth slowly relaxed. 'Make a note of this, Miss Jamieson. Miss Laura Jamieson and Mr Gideon Maitland will be married a week on Saturday.'

'Gideon, no!' she gasped. 'We can't—I can't——'

'We can, and you will,' he said arrogantly.

'I—I will?'

'Yes,' Gideon nodded. 'Unless you want to move in with me tonight?'

'No . . .'

He looked down at her teasingly. 'You don't sound too sure.'

Laura turned away. 'It isn't that.'

'Then what is it?' he frowned, an edge of uncertainty to his strong, masterful voice.

'You haven't even kissed me yet!' she told him in a disgruntled voice.

'Oh, Laura,' he chuckled throatily, 'you've just given me heaven. And I—I'm almost afraid to kiss you,' he admitted shakily.

'Afraid?' she echoed disbelievingly.

'Yes,' he groaned. 'What if I lose control?'

Delicate colour flooded her cheeks. 'What if you do?'

'We have to talk——'

She put her fingertips to his lips. 'We can talk later—much later. Now that I know you love me none of it seems important anyway.'

His face darkened. 'It was important enough to break us up.'

'It will still be there to be discussed *after* you've kissed me.' She looked up at him longingly.

'Will you be this demanding after we're married?' Gideon grinned, looking suddenly boyish.

Married! Just the thought of it gave her a warm glow. 'I hope so,' she smiled.

'God, Laura,' he gave a triumphant groan, 'I can hardly believe this is happening! After we parted earlier tonight I felt as if the world had come to an end.'

'Will you stop talking,' she said crossly. Much as she liked listening to the beautiful, wonderful things he was telling her, she would much rather feel his lips on hers, would much rather *know* his love. 'And kiss me,' she pleaded.

His mouth met hers in a kiss of hunger, slowly lowering her down his body to put her feet once more on the ground, moulding her pliant curves to the hardness of his body, only breaking the kiss to cover her face and throat with soft burning kisses.

'I love you, Laura,' he told her shakily. 'And no other woman has ever heard those words from me.'

She swallowed hard. 'They haven't?'

'Never.' His lips once more claimed hers, one of his hands claiming her breast, the other resting possessively on her thigh.

Their hunger for each other took some minutes to assuage, their caresses heated as they touched each other in rousing sensuality, until Gideon finally put her away from him, his eyes almost black as he looked at the disarray of her clothes, her breasts bared to his stimulating hands.

'Let's sit down,' he said gruffly.

Once on the sofa Laura moved eagerly into his arms, one of her hands entangled in his hair as she pulled his head down to her, their lips meeting in a show of mutual desire, her other hand resting on the nakedness of Gideon's chest, his shirt completely unbuttoned and pushed aside by her questing fingers.

'Make love to me, Gideon,' she pleaded.

'What do you think I'm doing now?' he asked raggedly.

'I want you completely.'

'Darling——'

'I want you, Gideon,' she said tearfully. He had roused her to such a pitch that she didn't want to stop now, wanted to continue to the nerve-shattering conclusion.

But Gideon was already moving away, fastening her blouse for her with unsteady fingers, a fine sheen of perspiration to his furrowed brow.

'Gideon——'

'I know, darling,' he cradled her roughly against his chest. 'But your mother is in her bedroom——'

'Then let's go to your house. Oh—of course, Lisa is there.' She looked down awkwardly at her hands.

Gideon gently raised her chin, looking steadily into her eyes. 'Lisa is Natalie's nanny, nothing else.'

'I don't like her,' Laura mumbled.

He gave a rueful smile. 'I think the feeling is mutual.'

'When we're married—when we're married will Lisa still live with us?' She looked up at him searchingly, believing him when he said the other woman meant nothing to him, but knowing that Lisa Harlow didn't feel the same way about him.

'Do you want her to?'

'No,' she replied without hesitation.

He frowned. 'There's Natalie——'

'I'll take care of her myself.'

Gideon gave a deep sigh. 'I think the time has come for that talk,' he moved to sit in the chair opposite, 'and I can think better when I can't touch you.'

Laura blushed at his admission of lack of control. 'Maybe we should talk,' she nodded.

'I think I should tell you about Felicity first.'

'Yes,' she agreed huskily, tearing her gaze reluctantly away from his rakish attractiveness.

'But before that I have to know you believe I love you,' he said intently.

He would never show such vulnerability if he didn't. 'I believe you,' she told him softly, her eyes glowing with her own love for him. 'I love you,' she added in case there were any doubts in his mind.

'You said you didn't,' he said with remembered pain.

'No, I didn't. I just challenged the statement, *you* took it to mean I no longer loved you.'

'An assumption you were quite happy to let me believe.' He gave her a reproving look.

She gave him a cheeky smile, sobering as she remembered they had yet to talk about his dead wife. 'Felicity,' she prompted.

'Yes,' he acknowledged reluctantly. 'I went to live with James and Felicity when I was sixteen. I suppose I had what you might call a crush on her at the time. But she was one of those girls who mature early, and I—well, I was a bit of a slow starter.'

'I'd never have believed it,' Laura teased to ease his tension.

'You're the recipient of twenty years' experience,' he mocked, laughing as she blushed. 'Anyway,' he was suddenly serious once more, 'Felicity knew of my infatuation, and she took great pleasure in teasing me. Then James sent me away to university. I gained self-confidence there——'

'Experience, you mean.'

'Okay, experience,' he shrugged.

'Was Lisa one of these experiences?'

'Yes,' Gideon sighed. 'We went out together for several months. But when I left university all that stopped. I went back to James's house——'

'To Felicity.'

'Yes. But in my maturity I could now see her for what she was, what James never saw, that she was a shallow butterfly of a woman incapable of feeling deep love for anyone but herself. Oh, she enjoyed trying to make me fall in love with her, increasingly so as it became obvious I wasn't interested. Unfortunately James had taken it into his head that the two of us should marry.'

'But you didn't have to do it!' Laura cried.

'No,' he agreed heavily. 'But at the time I couldn't see any real reason why I shouldn't. I didn't love anyone else, and physically we were very compatible. Oh yes,' he said bitterly at her gasp, 'Felicity and I had been lovers by this time.'

'So you married.' Laura wanted to get past the bit where Gideon had enjoyed sleeping with Felicity as soon as possible.

'Not immediately, no. I tried to persuade James that Felicity wouldn't be happy with me. Contrary to what some people believe, sex isn't everything in a marriage. Admittedly when that turns sour it rocks the whole marriage, but it shouldn't be the sole basis for any marriage. Unfortunately James had a heart attack shortly after this—you knew about his heart?'

'He told us,' Laura nodded.

'In a way I felt responsible. He wanted me to marry Felicity so much—a cementing of his old partnership with my father, I expect. *That's* when I married her.'

'Out of guilt and duty.'

Gideon gave a bitter half-smile. 'I wish I could say that, but it wouldn't be completely true. I enjoyed making love to Felicity. She was beautiful, a lovely asset for a young man just starting out in his career. People always liked Felicity, she was totally able to fit into any surroundings, could converse with any type of person. She was also an incredible actress,' he added bitterly. 'In public she would act such a loving wife that even I could almost believe it at times. In private—well, our marriage was a mockery of the word. I went into it intending to be faithful even if I didn't love her. Felicity—well, God knows why she married me. There were other men almost from the first.'

'Then Martin——'

'Just another in a long line of them. You remember I tried to tell him that the other week, but he wouldn't listen. He truly believed Felicity intended marrying him, whereas I know it never even entered her head. They were just an amusement to her, all of them. She took great enjoyment in telling me all about them. Needless to say, our own physical relationship was at an end, and had been for years.'

Laura was shocked by what he was telling her, she would be lying if she said she wasn't, but she needed to know. 'Why did you stay with her if you were so unhappy?'

He shrugged. 'I think it would have killed James to know what she was really like. He idolised her.'

'And were you—did you——'

His gaze sharpened. 'Did I what?'

'Did you have other women?' She steadily met his gaze.

'You mean Lisa, don't you?' he rasped.

'I mean any woman.'

'No.'

'You mean——'

'I mean no,' Gideon repeated harshly. 'My marriage vows happened to mean something to me. Felicity could have all the lovers she wanted, I worked to fill my time.'

It would explain the grimness he was reputed to have had over the years. 'When she died . . .?'

'There were other women then, a lot of them. I had a man's normal appetites, and they'd been repressed for too long. Then I met a young girl called Laura Jamieson,' he added softly, 'and none of those other women mattered any more.'

'Really?' she said shyly.

'Yes, really,' he smiled.

'I—Did James ever know about Felicity?'

'I hope not,' Gideon grimaced. 'No, I'm sure he didn't.'

'So Martin really meant nothing to Felicity,' she said sadly, knowing how hurt her brother would be if he knew the truth.

'No more than any of the other men.'

Laura couldn't understand any woman wanting other men when she had Gideon, and she said so.

His mouth twisted wryly. 'I think you could be biased.'

'Not at all—well, maybe a little. If loving you to distraction can be called bias.'

His eyes darkened in colour. 'It's called heaven. I'll show it to you, darling, as soon as you're my wife.' He saw Laura's frown. 'What is it?' he asked sharply.

'I don't understand why you offered Martin money when you knew he really meant nothing to Felicity— unless it was to save James pain. Was that it?' she asked eagerly.

'I repeat, I did not offer Martin money,' Gideon told her harshly.

'But——'

'I did not offer him fifty thousand pounds,' he repeated coldly.

'Then who——'

'I have no idea.' He was suddenly withdrawn from her.

'Oh, Gideon, I'm sorry!' Laura stood up to go to him,

kneeling in front of him on the carpeted floor. 'Martin must have been mistaken.'

'Yes,' he said tautly.

'Forgive me?' she looked at him pleadingly.

Gideon bent down and pulled her up on to his lap. 'Of course you're forgiven,' he smiled, although it didn't reach the bleakness of his eyes.

But his kiss held nothing back, and Laura knew the incident was forgotten, by Gideon at least. Lisa Harlow's name came into her mind in connection with the money Martin had mentioned, although why she suspected the other woman, and what her motive could have been, she had no idea. But she remembered Lisa saying she had money, and she knew the other woman wouldn't hesitate to use it, to use anything, to get Gideon. Who knew how Lisa Harlow's devious mind worked, or could even begin to guess her reasons for wanting Martin out of Felicity's life.

But she knew Gideon to be innocent in the matter, and returned his kiss with fervour. The smile they shared when their lips parted was in complete accord.

'Now we get to the part where Laura Jamieson entered my life.' Gideon's eyes twinkled down at her mischievously; he was totally relaxed now, his arm about her waist as he held her on his knees.

'Do you even remember our first meeting?' She knew she did, knew she had fallen in love with him then. But she doubted she had had the same effect on him.

Gideon soon disabused her of that fact! 'Of course I remember it,' he said indignantly. 'How could I forget the fiery-haired nineteen-year-old who was trying to look as old as Dorothy?'

'Oh, I wasn't trying to look that old—I mean—Oh, poor Dorothy!' she scowled at Gideon. 'I didn't mean to sound derogatory about her age.'

'Neither did I,' he chuckled. 'But a girl's age, or lack of

it, doesn't detract from her secretarial skills.'

She pulled a face at him. 'I know that, but you didn't have the trouble getting a job that I did. By dressing as I did I looked more the part.'

His mouth quirked. 'I think you overdid it, my love.'

'And that's the reason you remember me,' she said moodily.

'No,' Gideon chuckled, 'I remember you because of your fantastic figure. When you walked in with that tray of coffee I was admiring you from behind, wondering what the face was like to go with that beautiful body. When you turned round . . .!'

'You were disappointed,' she sighed.

'Disappointed is the last thing I was.' He shook her gently. 'I was bowled over. I took one look at you and fell in love with you.'

'You didn't!' she gasped. 'You couldn't have.'

'But I did.'

'But so did I—fall in love with you, I mean,' she explained excitedly. 'But I—You didn't seem all that interested,' she frowned.

'When you told me your name was Jamieson it was too much of a coincidence for you not to have been related to Martin. Checking up in your file confirmed it. Getting involved with my wife's ex-lover's sister was not something I wanted to do. But I couldn't seem to stay away from you, I even followed you home from work one evening. When you came out of the building a few minutes later looking like the teenager you are I cursed myself for a fool. Then James arranged for you to be my temporary secretary.'

'I dreaded it,' Laura recalled ruefully. 'I felt sure you would guess how I felt about you.'

'Well, I didn't. If I had have done perhaps I wouldn't have been such a bully to you. That first day, when Nigel came up to the office, seeing the way he talked to you, your response to him, I knew I didn't have any time to waste in getting you to agree to go out with me.'

'So you bulldozed me into it!'

Gideon nodded. 'You were so stubborn, so determined that you couldn't go out with your boss, that bullying you seemed the only way.'

'James absolutely loved that,' she said dryly.

'Yes,' Gideon grinned. 'It was the way he would have behaved himself. And he liked you, liked your spirit.'

'I doubt he would have approved of the way you suggested I become your mistress,' she reminded him reprovingly.

'I don't approve of it now either,' he scowled. 'But you frightened the life out of me.'

'*I* did?' Her eyes were wide.

'Mm,' he nodded. 'I told you I've never loved anyone else—well, loving you wasn't something I enjoyed. It weakened me, made me vulnerable to you. So I suggested the affair to get you out of my system. You rejected the idea without a second thought, even offered me back your resignation. And by making the suggestion at all I'd ruined your trust in me. Somehow I had to regain that trust.'

'Is that why you didn't kiss me all week?'

'Yes.'

'I hated that. I thought you didn't find me attractive.'

He raised his eyes heavenwards. 'There's no pleasing some women!'

'What changed your mind? I seem to remember a very passionate kiss in your office,' she blushed.

'Mm, that was Nigel Jennings' fault again. He was always hanging around you. I was terrified you were going to agree to go to the Company dinner with him.'

'So you arrogantly said I was going with you.'

'When I thought I'd ruined things again. You were so angry. Then you were jealous of Petra when you heard me talking to her on the telephone,' he smiled smugly. 'God, I felt good at that moment! Seeing you with Nigel had made me burn with jealousy, knowing you felt the same way about Petra gave my ego a boost.'

'And then you went away for a week.' Laura could still remember the loneliness of that time.

'What a hell of a week that was,' he groaned. 'I was in one meeting after another, longing to pick up the telephone and talk to you, but knowing it would only make my longing to see you worse.'

Laura glowed with the explanation of his silence for that long week. 'I missed you too.'

She received a long lingering kiss for her admission. Then Gideon scowled down at her again. 'When I did get back you were with Nigel Jennings again.'

'I was with James,' she corrected. 'Nigel had just asked me to dance, that was all.'

'Whatever your reason for being with him I didn't like it,' he muttered. 'I was pretty desperate by the time we reached your home that night. I would have made love to you if Martin hadn't been here.'

'And I would have let you,' she admitted huskily. 'I wanted you too.'

'You didn't after Martin had dropped his little bombshell.' Gideon looked bleak.

'Poor Martin,' she said softly. 'Someone should tell him the truth.'

'Not you, darling.' His arms tightened about her. 'Besides, from what you told me, he isn't exactly pining away.'

'You mean the other women he sees? But——'

'That's enough, darling,' he silenced her gently. 'Let's think of us now. We've done all the talking that's necessary.'

'Yes,' and she snuggled against him.

'Do you realise it's almost two o'clock in the morning?'

he murmured into her hair.

'Who's worried?' She kissed his throat.

'Not me,' he growled. 'But I've heard your new boss is a bit of a tyrant,' he added teasingly.

'Where did you hear that?'

'Someone mentioned it,' he smiled down at her.

'I'm surprised anyone dare *mention* it,' Laura murmured softly.

'This someone dares. It was your boss's boss.'

'Oh, James,' she nodded. 'Oh well, I needn't worry about my new boss being a tyrant to me,' she told him smugly.

Gideon quirked an eyebrow. 'Why's that?'

She sat up to rest provocatively on his chest. 'I know exactly how to—get round him.'

'You do?' he laughed softly.

'Oh yes.'

'Perhaps you could give me a—demonstration?'

'Gladly,' she grinned.

It was almost two-thirty before Gideon insisted he would have to leave. 'But I'll take you to work in the morning?' He stood up to button his shirt.

'I think I may just float there.' Laura gazed up at him adoringly.

'You too?' he grinned, very dark and attractive as he bent to kiss her parted lips. He only drew back far enough to look at her, his hands cupping either side of her face. 'You won't let anything change your mind about marrying me? Not Martin? Not anything?'

'No.'

'Promise?' he persisted.

'Yes,' she agreed easily, in such a state of euphoria that she was sure nothing could break them up now.

CHAPTER TEN

ONLY Laura's mother and James were told of their forth-coming marriage, the two of them having decided that Saturday's wedding was enough of a sensation at the moment. Time enough to tell of their own marriage when they got back from their honeymoon.

Laura's mother and James had made arrangements to come back from their honeymoon to attend the wedding, making no complaint about the haste of the wedding, rather they both encouraged it.

Laura was still working for James. She was to leave Courtneys the day before she was married, and a girl from the typing-pool was being trained as Gideon's new secretary. Laura teased him about the girl's obvious adoration.

'Maybe you should have become my secretary after all,' he said ruefully a few days later as they spent a quiet evening together at his home.

She smiled. 'I think you're quite safe with Marie.'

'So do I.' He grimaced. 'I'm not sure I'll be able to take her lisping much longer!'

Laura punched him playfully, curled up on the sofa beside him as they listened to the stereo after putting Natalie to bed. 'Don't be cruel!'

'I'm not,' he sighed. 'It's just that her girlish adoration can be very wearing.'

'She's older than I am!'

'You'd never know it. Every time I talk to her she looks at me with those devoted blue eyes. It's very unnerving.'

'Poor Gideon,' she taunted.

'Poor you, you little wretch.' He pulled her roughly

against him to kiss her hard on the mouth.

'Gid—Oh,' Lisa Harlow stood in the doorway, 'I didn't mean to—interrupt,' she said sweetly, her expression scathing as she watched Laura's selfconscious straightening of her clothes. 'There's a telephone call for you, Gideon. In your study.'

'Sorry, darling,' he smiled at Laura, standing up. 'I shouldn't be long.'

Lisa Harlow made no move to leave the room once Gideon had gone to his study, slowly closing the door to turn and face Laura. 'You think you've been very clever, don't you?' she hissed vehemently.

Laura steeled herself not to be affected by this woman's hate. It was only to be expected that she should be feeling resentful. 'If you think so,' she agreed calmly.

'Don't use that patronising tone to me!' Lisa sneered. 'You may think you've got rid of me, but you'll find you're the one to go!'

It was obvious that Gideon had told the other woman that her services at Natalie's nanny wouldn't be needed in a few weeks' time. 'Lisa——' Laura began.

'You won't marry him,' the other woman said confidently. 'I can guarantee that.'

Lisa's certainty made her shiver. She stood up. 'I understand you're upset about being parted from Natalie——'

'I'm not upset, Laura,' she scorned. 'Because I'm not going to be parted from her. And when I'm her stepmother I'll get someone in to care for the brat. I never did like children.'

Any guilt Laura might have felt about having the other woman's employment terminated was instantly dispelled. If she could talk about Natalie in this way then she didn't deserve to have the care of her.

'You may as well accept that Gideon and I will be marrying a week tomorrow.' They had the licence already, and all the arrangements had been made. She had been amazed at the ease with which Gideon smoothed all their plans through. But then maybe that wasn't so amazing, he was that type of man.

'Will you?' Lisa smiled, an unpleasant smile that mocked. 'I don't think so.'

'You've said enough, Mrs Harlow,' Laura told her coldly. 'I'd like you to leave now.'

Lisa smiled again. 'I won't be the one leaving—you will. And I guarantee you won't be back. You see, Gideon hasn't been totally honest with you——'

'He told me the two of you were lovers—years ago.'

The other woman's mouth twisted. 'That wasn't what I meant about him not being honest with you.'

Laura looked startled. 'Then what——'

'Wait and see,' Lisa purred confidently.

'Wait and see? But——'

'Before your wedding next Saturday I'll utterly destroy your trust in Gideon. I'm looking forward to it,' and she softly left the room.

Laura was shaking with reaction, her face pale. She had known her first meeting with the other woman after Gideon had informed her of their impending marriage wouldn't be very pleasant, but she hadn't expected threats. And those threats had sounded genuine.

But they couldn't be. She and Gideon talked openly about everything now, and the night he had asked her to marry him they had cleared up all misunderstandings between them. No, it must just be that Lisa Harlow couldn't resist this last bitchiness, that she hoped to arouse uncertainty.

Well, she wouldn't be uncertain! She loved Gideon, and she knew without question that he loved her. He showed her with every glance, every touch, and she was surprised the whole of Courtneys couldn't see the electric current passing between them every time they were in the same room together.

But so far their secret had remained just that, although most people were aware of the fact that Laura would be leaving the company in a week's time. She hugged the thought of being Gideon's wife to herself, finding the next week stretching out in front of her.

Gideon came back into the room. 'James,' he derided. 'I think he's been struck with a case of pre-wedding nerves.'

'Really?' she laughed, unable to picture her future stepfather in the least nervous.

'He's panicking about whether or not he gave me the ring to take tomorrow,' Gideon grinned, stretching his long legs out in front of him as he rejoined her on the sofa. 'That's the third time today.'

'My mother is as bad,' Laura smiled, shaking off the feeling of foreboding Lisa Harlow had evoked with her threats.

His arm went about her shoulders. 'Am I being unfair to you by denying you all the excitement of a big wedding?' he frowned down at her, smoothing her brow with long, caressing fingers. 'I want you for my wife so badly that I've selfishly pushed this rushed wedding on you.'

'And I was just thinking how long a week can be,' she told him truthfully.

'You were?' he chuckled.

'I was,' she nodded.

She received a long lingering kiss; Gideon only broke off the caress when passion threatened to consume them. 'You go straight to my head,' he muttered.

'Your head?' she teased.

His mouth quirked. 'You're a shameless young lady. I've invited Nigel to the wedding, by the way,' he added seriously.

Her eyes widened. 'Is he coming?'

Gideon nodded. 'He's bringing Janice.'

'He is?' she gasped her surprise.

'Jealous?' He quirked a questioning eyebrow.

'You know I'm not!' she snapped her indignation. 'They'll probably be ideal for each other. How can you even suggest such a thing when you know how much I love—Gideon!' she cried her reproach as she saw he was laughing at her. 'It isn't funny,' she glared at him.

'I was only checking, darling,' he chuckled throatily. 'Nigel had given me a few nasty moments in the past. I thought you were going to marry him.'

'How could I even think about it when you're the only man I can see?'

'Show me, Laura,' he invited gruffly. 'Show me how much you love me.'

Her convincing took several minutes, and by that time they had completely forgotten anything but each other.

Laura cried at her mother's marriage to James, not out of any feelings of sadness, but because of the look of pride in James's face as he looked at his new wife. Her mother was as shy as any other blushing bride, looking beautiful in a cream silk suit, the frothy lace hat a perfect match in colour.

Laura sent the telegram to Martin after the ceremony had taken place, but as the days passed and no reply was forthcoming she decided he was letting the past die a quiet death.

It came as a great surprise to her, and Gideon too, she had no doubt, when they were presented with a carriage clock by the staff of the firm on the eve of their wedding. She was too overwhelmed to make any response, but Gideon rose to the occasion, and made a warm and witty speech accepting the lovely gift.

'I couldn't let you get away with it that easily,' Nigel teased her as she cleared her desk of all personal belongings.

'*You* told them?' she gasped.

'Guilty.' His eyes twinkled mischievously.

'And I thought you were a friend!' she pretended indignation, secretly thrilled with the first wedding gift she and Gideon had received.

Nigel sat down on the edge of her desk. 'I am. Why else would I agree to come to the wedding?'

She kissed him warmly on the cheek. 'I'm so glad you decided to come after all.'

He smiled cheerfully. 'I wouldn't miss it for anything. You certainly kept everyone guessing.'

'I kept *me* guessing too!'

'I know,' he grinned. 'By the way, did you know that Janice is just longing to get married and have kids?'

'Really?'

'Yes, really,' he chuckled.

'What a coincidence,' Laura said tongue-in-cheek. 'Don't forget to invite Gideon and me to the wedding.'

'You wouldn't have been doing some matchmaking, would you?' he quirked an eyebrow questioningly.

'Not me,' she shook her head.

'The maybe it was your fiancé.'

'Now would I do a thing like that to a fellow bachelor?' Gideon strode into the office.

'To get Laura back, yes,' Nigel said dryly.

Gideon just smiled, not denying or admitting the deed. 'Ready to leave, darling? I've had the car brought round.'

Nigel stood up. 'What time shall Janice and I be at the register office tomorrow?'

'Any time before two-thirty. Otherwise you'll be too late,' Gideon smiled down possessively at Laura. 'I'm not delaying my marriage to Laura for any reason.'

Nigel put out his hand. 'The best man won—the best man for Laura, anyway,' he added mockingly.

Gideon shook his head warmly. 'But maybe not for Janice, hmm?'

'Too soon to tell,' the other man shrugged. 'I may as well come down in the lift with you if you're leaving now.'

The sight that met Laura's eyes when they emerged from the building had her gasping with dismay. Gideon came to a stunned halt, and Nigel burst into amused laughter.

Gideon's car had been decorated with balloons and tissue paper, a huge sign attached to the back saying, 'Just Married'.

'You delayed us deliberately!' she accused Nigel, unsure of Gideon's reaction as he still stared at his car.

'Well . . .'

'I'd forgotten people still did things like this,' Gideon murmured, turning to smile at Nigel. 'I'm grateful to you. The gift, the car—it's made everything perfect. Laura?'

'I love it!' she laughed her relief. 'But do you think James will appreciate being met at the airport in it?'

'He'll love it too,' Gideon chuckled. 'It will make him feel like a teenager again.'

They drove straight to the airport without changing a single thing about the car, and received indulgent looks as they drove through the busy streets.

The older couple were glowing, deeply in love, their marriage obviously a happy one, so much so that apart from a dry comment of 'Ridiculous!' James didn't mention the decorations on the car.

Laura was living in James's house, had been since the wedding the previous week. All of them had decided it would be easier if she were married from there, the apartment given up, and her belongings packed up ready to be moved into Gideon's house.

She spent the evening quietly with her mother and James, wondering if Gideon was feeling as nervous as she was.

Her mother and James would be returning to Barbados on Sunday, and probably wouldn't be back for a month or so. Her own honeymoon with Gideon was being spent in Greece, because of Gideon's recent vacation it was necessarily a short one. Courtneys couldn't be left indefinitely by both Gideon and James. Laura didn't mind, she hadn't been concerned about going away at all; just being with Gideon, as his wife, being enough.

Her wedding day dawned bright and sunny, seeming to match her mood. A visit to the hairdressers took up most of her morning, her hair trimmed into a feathered style, looking perfect under the lace Juliet cap she was wearing with her white chiffon gown.

Her mother and James were to be their witnesses, and James was as nervous as any other father about to see his daughter married.

When the doorbell rang at one o'clock Laura went to answer it. The servants were busy in the kitchen preparing the food for the small reception to be held here, her mother and James were getting ready before her mother came to help her dress. Her bathrobe was perfectly adequate attire to answer the door, reaching almost down to the floor.

'Martin!' she gasped as she saw her brother standing outside. 'And Gideon,' she looked at his grim face. 'Darling, what is it?'

'I think we'd better come inside,' he said quietly. 'Your brother has something to tell you. To tell all of you.'

'I—Of course,' she frowned. 'Come in.'

'Could you get your mother and James?' Gideon requested.

Laura looked concernedly at her brother, at his pale, drawn face. 'Are you ill?' she asked anxiously.

'No, not ill,' he muttered. 'Look, let's just forget this, Maitland,' he spoke to Gideon.

'No.' Gideon's tone was firm.

'Look, I'll just get out. I'll——'

'No,' Gideon repeated. 'If the truth has to come out, and I think it must, then it has to be now, before I make Laura my wife.'

'What is it?' Laura cried. 'What's wrong?'

'Just get your mother and James, darling,' Gideon prompted gently. 'And remember, I love you.'

'I love you too,' she said dazedly. 'But I don't understand——'

'You will,' he assured her grimly.

Laura felt the foreboding returning from when Lisa Harlow had threatened her. She had pushed the threats to the corner of her mind, but suddenly she knew that whatever was about to happen here the other woman had had a hand in it.

Her mother was ecstatic about Martin being here, and James shook hands with him goodnaturedly. Whatever was making Gideon look so grim, and Martin look ill, her mother and James knew nothing about it.

'You shouldn't be here, Gideon,' her mother scolded. 'It's bad luck to see the bride before the wedding.'

His smile was strained. 'There may not be a wedding——'

'Gideon——'

'No wedding!' her mother's gasp interrupted her protest.

'Don't be silly, boy,' James snapped. 'Of course there's going to be a wedding.'

'Gideon?' Laura choked.

'Listen to what Martin has to say,' he told her distantly, his emotions completely under control.

'Well?' she turned to her brother.

Martin looked at Gideon. 'I'm willing to forget I ever knew, Maitland. You're good for her——'

'I thought so,' Gideon replied coldly. 'But Lisa has seen fit to tell you the truth.'

'Lisa!' Laura gasped. 'What does she have to do with this?'

'Everything,' her brother admitted heavily. 'God, she's a bitch! How you stopped yourself from hitting her, I'll never know,' he spoke to Gideon. 'Throwing her out was too good for her.'

'Tell them!' Gideon prompted harshly. 'Tell them what Lisa told you this morning. Tell them!'

Martin licked his lips nervously, looking at them all with reluctance. 'I—I'm Natalie's father,' his head rose in challenge. 'I'm Natalie's real father.'

CHAPTER ELEVEN

MARTIN'S announcement heralded silence, a stunned, shocked silence. A strange hush filled the room, the outside world was forgotten.

'It was you!' James gasped at last, a terrible greyness to his skin.

His wife was instantly at his side. 'How could you?' she turned on her son. 'How can you tell such lies?'

James closed his eyes, taking deep breaths of air into his starved lungs. 'He isn't lying, Joan,' he said shakily.

'Not lying?' she frowned. 'But I—How?'

'Your son was in love with my wife.' Gideon spoke for the first time since Martin had made his claim.

'And I thought she loved me,' Martin put in bitterly. 'Some joke!'

Laura licked her suddenly dry lips, wondering when this nightmare was going to end. 'You know the truth now?'

'Oh yes, Lisa told me everything. And she enjoyed every minute of it, the bitch.'

'Laura,' her mother's voice was sharp, 'did you know about—this?'

'Not all of it,' Gideon answered for her. 'This last part is as much of a shock to Laura as it is to you.'

But was it? Gideon had told her he had stopped sleeping with Felicity years ago, and he hadn't refuted that statement. Natalie had to have been conceived somehow, which pointed to her being another man's child. And Gideon had cared for her as if she were his own, had loved her in spite of himself. His reluctant love of the little girl was now explained.

'No, it isn't,' she said firmly, moving to his side to slide her hand into his. 'I admire you for what you've done,' she told him huskily. 'It can't have been easy.'

'You knew Natalie wasn't yours—all the time?' James gasped.

'Of course,' Gideon nodded. 'But how did you?' His eyes were narrowed in puzzlement.

The older man sighed heavily. 'Felicity told me.'

Now it was Gideon's turn to go pale. 'You knew—about her——'

'Other men?' James sighed. 'Not at first. It was because of her affair with a married man that I had my heart attack, but when she agreed to marry you I thought she was finally settling down. Oh, I realised the two of you weren't as happy as you could have been, but you put on such a good act in front of me that I had no idea of the true state of your marriage. I was a little concerned with the fact that you didn't have children, but then a lot of couples wait nowadays. Then Felicity came to me and told me she was pregnant.' He seemed to be far away, in the past, vividly remembering. 'She also told me that it wasn't yours, but that you were never to know.'

'Oh God!' Gideon groaned. 'I knew damn well it couldn't be mine. I hadn't touched her for years.'

'I can explain why Felicity did it,' Martin put in gruffly. 'She knew that if her marriage to you broke up her father would probably disinherit her too.'

James nodded. 'I threatened as much.'

'Felicity knew that if you were both trying to protect each other from being hurt the truth would never come out, that once the baby was born she could continue with her old life, leaving each of you thinking you were protecting the other.'

'I hate to admit this,' James said heavily, 'but my daughter was an evil little bitch.'

'Yes,' Martin finally seemed to have realised that.

'When Lisa told me about Natalie I—well, I admit I had some crazy idea of taking her back to the States with me.'

Gideon tensed at Laura's side. 'Never! In every way that matters she's my child.'

James shook his head. 'Gideon, you don't have to do this. I realise now that over the years you must have done things—things that can only have brought you un-happiness, to give me peace of mind over Felicity. But this is going too far——'

'Too far!' Laura was suddenly defending Gideon like a cat protecting her kitten, spitting and clawing at anyone who threatened to hurt him any more. She could feel his pain even now, feel it ripping him apart. 'Natalie is Gideon's child, she has been since the day she was born. And if we have to fight you for her in court, Martin, we will!'

'Darling——'

'Martin?' she prompted tautly, ignoring Gideon for the moment.

Her brother was looking at her in open-mouthed amaze-ment. Laura had never spoken to him like this before. 'Before Maitland made his objections I was about to say I know it wouldn't work out,' he said slowly. 'Natalie be-longs to him, I know that.'

'You should have taken the money when it was offered,' James said dully.

'Money?' Gideon's expression sharpened. 'What do you know about the money?'

'I was the one who offered it, boy. Not personally, of course. I had a lawyer deal with that.'

'It was you?' Laura gasped. James was the last person she would have thought of.

'Yes. I didn't realise it was to your brother, of course. I never knew the details, and especially not the identity of the baby's father. I had Felicity arrange it all with my lawyer. She was terrified the father would find out and spoil things for her.' He put his face in his hands. 'It was my fault she was like she was. When her mother died giving birth to her I spoilt her, gave her everything she ever wanted. And she turned out to be totally selfish, unable to love anyone but herself.'

Laura's mother took charge. 'Laura, could you please take everyone into the lounge. I want to be alone with James.'

'Joan——'

'I insist, James,' she said with some of her old independence. 'Laura, please.'

Laura's hand was still firmly in Gideon's when they got to the other room. 'Will you agree to a legal adoption?' she immediately demanded of her brother.

'Laura——'

'Gideon, please,' she looked at him lovingly. 'Natalie is ours, yours and mine, and Martin has no part of her. A brief affair doesn't make him a father.'

'You're right,' Martin agreed dully. 'In my own way I'm as bad as Felicity was. I thought I wanted to marry her, that I loved her, but if she had come to me and told me she was pregnant I doubt if I would have married her. I'm a bit like Dad was, Laura. I need a girl in every port. And I certainly couldn't bring a child up.'

'So you'll agree to the adoption?' Gideon asked deeply.

'Yes, I'll agree to anything you want. There's just one thing . . . I realise that both of you would rather not see me again, but I'd like to see Natalie occasionally. Just as an uncle,' he added hastily. 'If you would rather I didn't——'

'As long as it's only as an uncle I have no objections,' Gideon accepted.

Laura squeezed his hand before turning to her brother. 'Thank you,' she said deeply.

'Mum——'

'Will come round. Just give her time.'

Time—it was what they all needed.

A year can be a short time when you're ecstatically happy, and despite the upset on the afternoon of their wedding, Laura had been happy with Gideon every day of their marriage.

Natalie seemed to learn something new every day. Her newest trick was waking them up at six o'clock in the morning singing the latest nursery rhyme she had learnt.

Today the three of them were out to dinner. Natalie had been allowed up especially for the occasion. Not that she could possibly know the significance of the day, but her relieved parents did. Today Natalie officially became their child. Her adoption was complete, and her uncle Martin was a particular favourite with her.

Gideon raised his champagne glass. 'To at last being a family.'

'To us all,' Laura echoed, sipping the bubbly wine. 'It's a pity Mum and James couldn't be here to help us celebrate.' She helped Natalie with her orange juice.

'Now that we've finally got him to retire it's only natural they should want to go to America to spend some time with Martin, especially today. Any regrets, darling?' He looked at her anxiously, at her newfound maturity, the glow of love they both shared.

'None at all. You?'

'Only one—that we aren't anywhere where I can take you to bed.' His expression was sensual.

'Gideon!' she giggled, looking about them selfconsciously.

His hand covered hers. 'I hope you know how much I love you,' he said intently.

'I do,' she told him huskily.

'I had no idea how you were going to react to Martin being Natalie's father,' he said with remembered pain. 'I intended telling you after the wedding, and when he turned up . . . God, I thought I'd lost you.'

'You'll never lose me,' she assured him.

He looked at their daughter with tender eyes. 'It's good to know she's ours at last. I always thought Martin would came back one day, that he would find out about Natalie, and take her away from me.' His face was shadowed. 'I hardly dared to love her.'

'I know, darling,' she squeezed his hand. 'But it's all over now.'

He shook his head, smiling. 'It's only just beginning for us. I hope forty or fifty years will be long enough.'

'For what?' she frowned.

'To love you, to be loved by you, to just be with you,' he told her simply.

'We always have eternity.' Laura smiled tearfully at the depth of his love for her.

'I hope so,' he said fervently.

'We will, Gideon,' she vowed. 'We will.'

Harlequin Salutes... ANNE MATHER

The author whose romances have sold more than 90 million copies!

Harlequin is proud to salute Anne Mather with 6 of her bestselling Presents novels—

1 **Master of Falcon's Head** (#69)
2 **The Japanese Screen** (#77)
3 **Rachel Trevellyan** (#86)
4 **Mask of Scars** (#92)
5 **Dark Moonless Night** (#100)
6 **Witchstone** (#110)

Wherever paperback books are sold, or complete and mail the coupon below. ✱

Harlequin Reader Service

In the U.S.
P.O. Box 22188
Tempe, AZ 85282

In Canada
649 Ontario Street
Stratford, Ontario N5A 6W2

Please send me the following editions of Harlequin Salutes Anne Mather. I am enclosing my check or money order for $1.75 for each copy ordered, plus 75¢ to cover postage and handling.

☑1   ☑2   ☑3   ☑4   ☑5   ☑6

Number of books checked _____ 6 _____ @ $1.75 each = $ _____

N.Y. state and Ariz. residents add appropriate sales tax $ _____

Postage and handling $ .75

TOTAL $ __10.50__

I enclose __9$.25__
(Please send check or money order. We cannot be responsible for cash sent through the mail.) Price subject to change without notice.

NAME __maria PLACIDO__
(Please Print)
ADDRESS __53 Wyndham St.__
CITY __Toronto__
STATE/PROV. __Ontario__   ZIP/POSTAL CODE __M6K-1R9__

✱ Offer available beginning January 1983 and continuing as long as stock lasts!
Offer expires July 31, 1983

MATHER-SAL

30156000000

Readers rave about Harlequin romance fiction...

"I absolutely adore Harlequin romances! They are fun and relaxing to read, and each book provides a wonderful escape."
—N.E.,* Pacific Palisades, California

"Harlequin is the best in romantic reading."
—K.G., Philadelphia, Pennsylvania

"Harlequin romances give me a whole new outlook on life."
—S.P., Mecosta, Michigan

"My praise for the warmth and adventure your books bring into my life."
—D.F., Hicksville, New York

*Names available on request.

HELP HARLEQUIN PICK 1982's GREATEST ROMANCE!

We're taking a poll to find the most romantic couple (real, not fictional) of 1982. Vote for any one you like, but please vote and mail in your ballot today. As Harlequin readers, you're the real romance experts!

Here's a list of suggestions to get you started. Circle your choice, <u>or</u> print the names of the couple you think is the most romantic in the space below.

Prince of Wales/Princess of Wales

Luke/Laura (General Hospital stars)

Gilda Radner/Gene Wilder

Jacqueline Bisset/Alexander Godunov

Mark Harmon/Christina Raines

Carly Simon/Al Corley

Susan Seaforth/Bill Hayes

Burt Bacharach/Carole Bayer Sager

Prince of Wales of
(please print)
Prince ss of Wales
Luke/Laura.

Please mail to: Maureen Campbell
Harlequin Books
225 Duncan Mill Road
Don Mills, Ontario, Canada
M3B 3K9

POLL-1

Take these
4 best-selling novels
FREE

Yes! Four sophisticated, contemporary love stories by four world-famous authors of romance FREE, as your introduction to the Harlequin Presents subscription plan. Thrill to **Anne Mather**'s passionate story BORN OUT OF LOVE, set in the Caribbean.... Travel to darkest Africa in **Violet Winspear**'s TIME OF THE TEMPTRESS....Let **Charlotte Lamb** take you to the fascinating world of London's Fleet Street in MAN'S WORLD .... Discover beautiful Greece in **Sally Wentworth**'s moving romance SAY HELLO TO YESTERDAY.

Harlequin Presents...

The very finest in romance fiction

Join the millions of avid Harlequin readers all over the world who delight in the magic of a really exciting novel. EIGHT great NEW titles published EACH MONTH! Each month you will get to know exciting, interesting, true-to-life people .... You'll be swept to distant lands you've dreamed of visiting .... Intrigue, adventure, romance, and the destiny of many lives will thrill you through each Harlequin Presents novel.

Get all the latest books before they're sold out!
As a Harlequin subscriber you actually receive your personal copies of the latest Presents novels immediately after they come off the press, so you're sure of getting all 8 each month.

Cancel your subscription whenever you wish!
You don't have to buy any minimum number of books. Whenever you decide to stop your subscription just let us know and we'll cancel all further shipments.